A NOVEL

The Other Side
of the Fence

JULIE DEWEY

COPYRIGHT

Other books by Julie Dewey:
Forgetting Tabitha: The Story of an Orphan Train Rider
One Thousand Porches
The Back Building
Cat (Livin' Large Series)

If you like this book and
you wish to join my mailing list
for new releases, please visit my website
www.juliedewey.com or
log on to http://eepurl.com/DHWw9

"I know God will not give me anything I can't handle.
I just wish He didn't trust me so much."

Mother Teresa

CONTENTS

FAITH

JENNY

FAITH

JENNY

FAITH

JENNY

FAITH

JENNY

FAITH

DOROTHY

FAITH

INTRODUCTION

There is a fence that lurks between my former life and my current existence. A threatening, looming fence formed of cold metal chains and razor-sharp barbed wire. The erect enclosure serves as a reminder of my misfortune. I dare not attempt to climb it and be wounded, however, a brave few before me have hollowed out the ground beneath its surface and crawled under to escape, soiling their egos as well as their clothes. I follow their lead below the gate, through the dusty hole clawing my way to the other side.

On the other side of the fence my soul awakens, my body emerges fortified and willing, as if the water I run towards is a lover. A lover whispering softly, lulling me to undress before it and lunge into its depths with an urgency so deep the punishment won't matter.

My lover calls me towards its wide mouth. Stepping lightly through the swamp cabbage and cattails, mud oozes between my toes, enveloping and claiming me. I strip off my night clothes, my armor, and submerge myself deeper within the cold depths of the river; the murky water a tonic for my patchy, sticky, summer skin. I fill my lungs and vanish beneath the surface leaving only small ripples in my wake. My gloom descends as I plunge even deeper, striving to reach the bottom. Only when my lungs are deflated and in pain do I rise to the top and gasp for air. I settle into a rhythm with each gentle stroke and clear my head, remembering what it means to be alive. The water is a gift, a treasure, a world away from the misery and misfortune of the daytime.

When I step onto the riverbank, warm, thick air caresses my skin and keeps me company as I lay my diseased body upon the damp ground. Naked and exhausted the moon's reflection is my only earthly companion. The cool soil against the small of my back reminds me of the simple pleasures.

Insomnia grips me tightly with its gnarled, greedy hands so that I am no longer familiar with the profit of a dream's escape. I cast my gaze toward the heavens and count the stars that reflect like mirrors on the river. I dream, while awake, of yesterdays and my life as it used to be.

Echoes of the bullfrog's deep baritone mating call add to my dream and remind me of the symphonies I will never attend. My heart beats in rhythm with the frogs and cicadas, my pulse slows, and I become one with my surroundings. This is when I pray. I pray fervently for a cure so that I may go home once more and see my family again. I pray to reclaim my name and my status among my peers. I pray my patches will clear up never to return, and that the lack of sensitivity in my fingers improves. I pray for forgiveness and seek answers to the questions that plague me daily. What did I do to deserve this? Why me, Lord? I pray to be loved.

CHAPTER 2

VANISHING

1935

I have an ability to vanish and go unnoticed for long stretches of time. It's a rare gift that I have possessed since I was a small child. It's how I knew my father was having an affair with his secretary and how I knew my sister was the favorite child. It's also why my symptoms went undiscovered for so long. The pale patch of itchy skin on my forearm, followed by a loss of sensation in my fingertips, were my secrets alone for an entire débutante ball season. It was during a fitting for a new gown that my mother finally noticed my angry skin.

"Surely it's eczema, Darling. Still, I will make you an appointment with Dr. Manly for a colloidal silver ointment," she says with a brassy edge to her voice, as if she is being inconvenienced yet again by her oldest daughter.

"It hardly warrants an appointment, Mother. It doesn't itch," I lie. Mother is insistent and my fate becomes sealed. I had the rash for nearly six months and was treating it on my own with cool cloths at night and foundation and powders to cover it during the day.

The local family doctor assesses my condition and uses a knife like instrument to take a scraping of skin from my ear lobe, a procedure that I find odd. Within three days I am told I have a disease called leprosy and plans to evacuate me are quietly and discreetly put into place leaving me no time to say proper goodbyes.

"We don't want the townsfolk to know, Darling. We'll tell them you are visiting a distant relative for the time being. When you are cured, you will come home." Mother invents the excuse so that her life can continue to be enriched with material possessions and fine wine, while mine is being upended and stripped down. She shows little outward concern and fusses less than I expect. My sister, Emily, is told that our dear Aunt Esther, who resides in New York, is in need of my assistance. Emily stomps her feet and makes a big fuss that I am going to the city without her. If I didn't know better I would say her outbursts alarm my parents more than my repulsive condition and future confinement. When I leave the house for good, with only one small suitcase full of treasures, no one close to me or in my town is the wiser and my family's reputation remains intact. I thought my sister, at the very least, would question my sudden departure given that I have a suitor and it is still ball season. Instead, I won't be surprised if she delights in being the apple of our mother's eye now, her one and only showpiece to dress up and parade around town. Just the thought of it makes my blood boil.

I have to get word to William, my suitor, and tell him I have to go away for a short while. The thought of leaving him is heart wrenching, we are growing closer each day we spend together and I feel certain we have a future ahead of us. I write him a note explaining that I have to help my Aunt for a few months but that he will be in my heart the entire time I am gone, and until then, I hope I am in his as well.

The following day my father hires a car to take me to Carville. He leaves the house early in the morning without so much as a goodbye. My mother sips her tea beside me while I eat a plate of bland wet eggs and toast. She peruses the newspaper as if it were any other ordinary day and hushes me with a finger to her lips when I ask if she will visit or send care packages.

"You're old enough to manage, Frances. I expect you'll be home within a few months and you can pick up right where you left off, don't be difficult," she says.

"Oh, but what about William, Mother? I've written him a note and beg you to post it for me," I say, puffing out my lower lip.

"What about him, Dear? You'll need to forget about him for now," she says passively, knowing full well the extent of my feelings.

"Never mind," I say, feeling distraught. "I'll ask Emily to post it instead."

I am told to use a pseudonym and direct any correspondence to a P.O. box so the townsfolk don't uncover my true whereabouts. I am not to expect letters from home, for my mother is far too busy to respond.

The time has come for my departure. Mother pecks the air above my cheek, and stares at me a moment too long, this her only show of emotion, and pays the driver handsomely when he handles my bag. He opens the side door for me and I get settled. When the engine revs and we pull away from the curb I turn in my seat and glance out the back window to see if my mother is on the stoop watching me drive away, but she isn't. No one is.

***

The drive from my residence in Baton Rouge to Carville is precisely thirty-two miles. It's not long enough for me to get a grip on my anxiety. My stomach coils and my heart flutters wildly as we drive past stately homes and horse farms into the countryside where open fields are dotted with speckled dairy cows and lonely oak trees. Finally, we are on a winding dirt road that parallels the Mississippi River, aptly named, River Road, and I know we are nearing my destination. The road is riddled with bumps and divots that have me bouncing off my seat as our car spews dust behind us.

"Pardon me, Ma'am, I am not at liberty to drive you any further," the driver says.

I notice a closed gate ahead and a sign that reads: National Leprosy Hospital of the United States. U.S. Marine Hospital #66.

The driver stops the car and comes around to open my door. It's a kind gesture that I will never forget because this man, who is a stranger to me, still treats me like I am a lady. He bows his head and tips his hat towards me as I lift my small suitcase, inhale deeply, and prepare to meet my fate. I stare, seeing massive trees draped in moss line the pathway in front of me to the administration building where I have to go and check in.

An apparition in white floats towards me with arms outstretched like wings. Her pallor is so luminescent that if she wore a halo I would mistake her for an angel.

"Hello," she calls out and motions me inside, the inflections in her voice soft and soothing enough to erase some of my fear and tension. I move slowly forward and the gate swings shut behind me. I hear that same clinking sound as the gate locks behind me, imprisoning me.

CHAPTER 3

ANGELS

I put my suitcase down and look over my surroundings. I notice small cottages, large buildings, and a covered corridor that connects them all. The surroundings are peaceful and pretty enough I decide, but then the reality of my circumstance sets in and anxiety creeps into my body once more, courses through my veins, and steals my breath.

"Hello there," I say in return to the wonder in my presence.

"My name is Sister Catharine. I am a nurse here. I am part of the Sisters of Charity order from New Orleans. I promise I will take good care of you. First we are going to the administration building over there to check in." The woman hugs me, her arms wrap tightly around my slender body cradling me in her embrace. She smells of honeysuckle and pain. I stifle the urge to cry, goosebumps appear on my skin and I clutch my arms together and remember this is the time to be strong. I am pensive for a moment and then gather my courage and look into the eyes of Sister Catharine and introduce myself.

"I am Faith," I say. My new name feels adverse on my tongue, thick and cumbersome rather than light and airy and full of hope as it implies.

***

I am housed in a former slave cabin that has been enlarged and converted into a sizable cottage. There are eleven other women of varying ages who reside in the building with me. My room is sparse and unwelcoming, there is nothing but a few yards of drab muslin across my window sill to keep the sunlight out in the early morning hours.

The house is tidy enough, but there are no comforts of home. There aren't any fluffy pillows to lounge upon or soft carpets to walk across. There aren't even billowy curtains to add color and appeal to the front windows. There is a bathroom in the hallway, a small kitchen area and a place for sitting. This evening, however, no one is around and the space feels as empty and barren as my heart. The seconds tick by; it is true, time does not stand still. Yet, while I take in my new surroundings and breathe in my new life it hardly seems as if anything will ever be the same. The morning hours of my life are lost forever, spent eating runny eggs and burnt toast with a reticent mother who paid me no mind.

One thing I have to force myself to acknowledge about mother is that when she acts as if nothing is the matter, there usually is. How can my mother pretend nothing is wrong when her own child has been sent away to a prison for having committed no crime? This sudden epiphany makes me feel even more afraid and alone.

I will rest and pray, eat and pray, and then pray again until I am well. Then I will go home to William and we will begin our life together. Surely he has received my letter by now and will understand that I have a family obligation. I have no doubt that he will wait for my return in a few months. Until then, I vow to keep my head held high and make the most of my situation. I am certain I am here for a reason, for that is the way of things. Although why I have been singled out for this torturous road I do not understand. We all have lessons to learn and surely modesty is one of mine.

CHAPTER 4

HUMBLED

Upon my arrival at Carville, I am humbled by the open arms and welcoming nature of the staff and patients. People are not afraid to embrace and show emotion, in fact they wear it on their sleeves. I coil at the sight of all this suffering and ask God for forgiveness because I know these poor souls are in despair and they didn't ask to have leprosy. But some people I pass are hideously misshapen or, God forgive me, simply hideous. Am I to live with these people?

My first hours at the hospital are spent checking in at the record room. A lady by the name of Bridget welcomes me and takes my history.

"My name is Faith Cooper. I am eighteen years old and I am from New Orleans, Louisiana," I lie. I take William's last name for my own without his permission but I like the twangy sound of 'Cooper' and I expect it to be my name one day anyway. I have been to extravagant balls in New Orleans and long to live among the hustle and bustle of the city so I insert that desire into my history as well.

"Faith, now that is a lovely name," Bridget nods in approval and scribbles it on the form.

"Thank you," I say, feeling uncomfortable but as if I have made a good choice.

"The dinner bell rings at eleven and the supper bell rings at five o'clock. When you've finished your meal this evening, you will meet with the executive officer, Dr. Jo. He'll examine you and explain how things work here at Carville. In the morning you will see the dentist and have your labs drawn. We will also need to vaccinate you against smallpox. It's a painstaking process but the Sisters will help you get oriented, you will find your place, don't worry, Dear. Why you look frightened to death," she says and places a gentle hand on mine for a brief moment.

"It's overwhelming," I admit.

"One step at a time," Bridget advises.

"Thank you for your kindness."

"You know, Mother Teresa once said, "God doesn't require us to succeed; he only requires that you try."

"Thank you, I'll keep that in mind," I think about the quote and promise to try to get along here, what other choice do I have?

I like Bridget, she is warm and appears unscathed. I remind myself whether or not she is afflicted, we are all the same in God's eyes.

I stroll into the dining hall and appreciate the familiar smells wafting from the kitchen. Buttermilk fried chicken and biscuits are on the menu and I suddenly realize I am near starving. My eggs turned my stomach this morning and I skipped dinner at eleven all together. Looking around at the inhabitants of the cafeteria my stomach lurches and my appetite wanes instantly. All I see are rotting limbs everywhere I look.

It is obvious that the patients with white opaque eyes or those wearing eye patches are blind. They wait patiently to be spoon-fed and cared for and receive both grace and empathy from the Sisters. Everywhere I look I see lepers and the startling image of suffering. How can I be among this scarred group? Disfigured patients in wheelchairs line the hallway, some are missing limbs, others have appendages wrapped in bandages with blood seeping through. Some people are so disfigured from the pustules and rashes covering them you can hardly make out their faces. I am torn between the desire to flee at once and the Christian obligation to help those less fortunate.

I recoil when I see a woman without a nose, she has a hole where her membranes should be and a puss like substance runs out from her orifices. Not far from her is a man with no upper lip who slurps his tea carefully with his head tilted backwards, liquid dribbles down his chin. Children are present as well, some with skin so riddled and ripe with lesions I can only imagine the pain it causes them. Several patients are covered in purple ointment, it must be a salve of some sort to treat their condition. People scratch at skin patches with stumps and cry out in agony. Yet, other patients, who are clearly affected, carry on as if nothing at all is wrong. Voices carry and silverware clangs as folks enjoy their sustenance and treat one another with kindness.

The visual of puss streaming down the faces of several patients combined with the smell of rotting flesh fills the air and mixes with the cooking smells and antiseptic. I am terrified this is going to happen to me, and my stomach tightens at once.

I am not able to take in the sight of so much human indignity and run from the dining hall, down the slight hill to my cottage. I grab my toiletries and hurry to the bathroom where I wretch until I am dry heaving and have exhausted myself completely. I brush the vomit from my teeth and rinse and spit. This place is hell on earth but surely I am awake for when I pinch my forearm forcefully it turns purple and throbs.

***

"I understand you have not eaten yet, here is a biscuit and some cold chicken, it's important to get proper nutrition." The executive officer, Dr. Frederick Andrew Johansen, positions a plate before me and urges me to eat. However, the mottled fried chicken skin reminds me of the lesions I saw covering several patients' faces and I am not able to take a bite.

"Call me Dr. Jo," the man says, "I am the attending doctor here at Carville and I don't want you to worry, I'll see to it that you are well taken care of."

"Pleased to meet you, Dr. Jo," I say offering my hand.

"I hope your accommodations are satisfactory?" he asks.

"They are fine, I only expect to be here for a short while so I can make do for now."

"Ahh, I see. Let's get on with your case then and we'll start your treatments right away."

The doctor is warm and friendly and I feel calm in his presence. He explains that the best treatment at this time is a prescription of two weekly injections of chaulmoogra oil along with a few drops of chaulmoogra oil capsules with each meal.

"I've never heard of this oil, what is it and where does it come from?" I ask, skeptical.

"The oil is widely used in Indian cultures as well as being a traditional Chinese medicine. It comes from a deciduous tree indigenous to India that bears velvety fruit from August to September. The large seeds contain a fatty oil that when expressed produces a brown liquid. I'll warn you now that the odor is unpleasant and the taste is sharp and pungent, but it has proved to be effective for skin ailments."

"Okay," I say feeling as if I have little choice but to take the medicine and pray it gets me out of here soon.

"The breakfast bell rings at seven a.m., and morning mass is at eight a.m.. We have two churches on campus one is Protestant and one is Catholic. Seventy-five percent of our population is Catholic and I see here that you are as well, correct?"

"Yes, Sir, I am," I acknowledge even though right now I am angry with God.

"The Catholic Chapel has mass in the evening at seven, as well as in the morning, and you may attend both if you like."

"Thank you, I am sure I will find my way. Doctor, may I ask how many patients have been released from Carville?"

"My goodness, that's a complicated question indeed. If you have a verified case of leprosy as you do, I am afraid it's the law that keeps you here under quarantine. Yes, we have had one or two folks that have left, one escaped and the other was deemed well enough to go. I am bound by patient confidentiality and am unable to give you the details but let's say the diagnosis was debatable at best. Faith, Carville is a place like no other. I have watched it grow from a leper home to a hospital over the years and, people adapt, they find joy and live peaceful lives. You are young and ambitious and have a lifetime ahead of you so I advise being hopeful. The patients here are grateful they have a safe place to live out their days without harsh judgment or penalties from the outside world."

"That sounds ominous to me, do you mean I will never be able to leave here, ever?" I ask, knowing I am different from the other patients. I feel that I am above the other folks here because I have so few outward scars.

"All we can do is take our medicine and practice kindness; many folks pray as well. I pray everyday to understand this disease and someday we will, until then you will remain here, I'm sorry."

"Thank you, Doctor," I say just to be polite as he shows me out from his office. I am seething that so many people think I belong here when I am clearly different than the others. I walk back through the cold, covered corridor, through the dining hall, and outdoors to my cottage. When I arrive two of my housemates are in the sitting room.

"Hello, I am Faith," I introduce myself.

"I'm Evelyn, welcome," an older woman with puffy, red-rimmed eyes introduces herself.

"Welcome, Faith. I am Marilyn, would you care to join us for the movie tonight? They're showing The Broadway Melody, it's part musical, part romance."

"Golly. I am tuckered out from the day, I think I will turn in early. Thank you for the invitation though, perhaps I can join you next time." Marilyn is slightly deformed, her right arm is bandaged but she has use of her left and seems to make do. My housemates are warm and kind but I am not afflicted as they are.

I collect my toilet items and brush my teeth thoroughly to get ready for my dentist appointment tomorrow. I brush too hard and blood tinges my spittle in the sink. I rinse carefully so no one thinks I am messy. I splash cool water on my face and sit to tinkle. I am grateful for the indoor plumbing and as I make my way to my room I am grateful for a mattress as well. It could be worse I suddenly realize and feel overwhelmed by the thought of the patients that came before me to lesser conditions when the cottages were rustic, inhospitable slave cabins. I vow to study this disease and learn everything I can about it so that I will be one of the few released. I am young and otherwise healthy, I must have hope, and as I close my eyes I dream of my future for what is more hopeful than that?

In the morning I rise with the sun. I dread getting out of bed but force my tired arms to throw back my coverlet and expose my flawed naked skin to the air. The bathroom is occupied so I dress in my room and walk to breakfast alone. Picturesque oaks with wide sweeping branches and peeling bark tower over the pathway.

I eat a simple breakfast of fruit and dare not avert my eyes from my bowl. In order to be strong I need to keep my food down. I realize I am a leper like the other people here but I am better off than they are with just a few patches of flaky skin and minor numbness. I am not able to take in the horrors of the place yet. When I finish my meal I walk across the boardwalks to church.

I grasp my rosary in my hand and pray for courage because I will need it to get through the day.

I have time alone before my dental appointment and use it to explore my surroundings. I have been told that Carville sits on nearly four hundred acres. There are pecan groves, gardens, crops, land set aside for the grazing animals, as well as fields for ball games and recreation. I am surprised to learn there is even a post office, bakery, and laundry facilities.

The Mississippi River is along the east side of the facility and there is a lake across campus that patients can use for recreational activities like fishing and canoeing.

Sturdy, yet well worn benches have been placed thoughtfully beneath the trees in order to provide shade. I see women seated together on one side of the campus and men in groups on the other. I have been advised that mingling of the sexes is frowned upon here at Carville for a variety of reasons. I don't have to stretch my imagination too far for when William kissed me the first time, my body burned with fever in places I hadn't known had feeling. Still it seems an indignity to me that the sexes should be kept apart at all times, just as it is an indignity that the afflicted use a separate chalice during church for communion; after all, doesn't that wine become God's blood? How could that be infected? I have to adapt, but my heart remains guarded. I am not here to form bonds and friendships, I am here to get well and return home. My focus will be on that alone, I will walk the perimeter of the grounds to maintain my strength, perhaps I might even take part in the field days, but in my spare time I plan to read and rest, study and learn how to adapt until I am able to be with my loved ones once again.

CHAPTER 5

APPOINTMENTS

My first appointment of the day is with the resident dentist, a burly fellow with a thick beard. He scrapes plaque from my teeth and pokes my gums with a sharp instrument. He tells me my gums are slightly swollen and receding but that my teeth are cavity free. The dentist prescribes a saltwater rinse twice daily to help my gums achieve optimal health and prevent the loss of any of my teeth. He also suggests that I irrigate my nose daily. I tell him I clench my jaws so tightly at night that I fear I will break my teeth but he assures me there are no cracks at this time and if I develop further problems not to hesitate to see him.

My next stop is the laboratory near the infirmary. My skin is scraped with a knife and my tissue is smeared onto a glass slide for scrutiny under a microscope. I find it curious that skin is scraped from my ear lobe again. The lab assistant explains that the disease often hides beneath the lobe itself and finally I nod in understanding. The lab assistant pricks my veins with a needle and draws blood for testing, then he pokes my finger and smears more blood onto glass slides. I am bandaged and directed to my next appointment with the head nurse who is waiting for me in the operating room.

The head nurse is required to inoculate all patients with a vaccination for smallpox to prevent an outbreak. I tell her I was inoculated as a small child by our family's physician and show her my inoculation scar on my upper arm. Luckily, I have been poked and prodded enough for the week. I am told that my results will be studied and charted and in a few weeks I will meet with several more doctors from varying fields of study for follow-up exams.

The morning has rushed by and the eleven a.m. dinner bell

is ringing already. The women I met from my humble cottage call my name and invite me to sit among them for the meal. I am grateful for the company and join them at once. I introduce myself to the other women from my cottage and learn that it is normal for cottage groups to eat and go to social activities together. Luckily my group is comprised of friendly and warm women, all of whom are only mildly affected with leprosy. Some women in my group have claw-like hands, and others have deformed ears, one even appears to be losing her vision. Her eyes are murky and dilated, but still, this crowd is far better off than many here.

I pray before I eat my food; "Dear Lord, I thank you for this meal before me. I pray it is used to give me sustenance so that I may have the strength and will to heal and help those around me. Amen." When I raise my head, I note that several women are still deep in prayer, I hesitate to eat until everyone is ready. The meal is generous and flavorful. Another thing to be grateful for. I pinch my sweet roll off in sections and swallow it down with frothy milk; I can do this I remind myself.

During dinner conversation I learn that several of my house-mates have resided at Carville for more than half their life. When I tell them I have been given a lighter diagnosis and expect to be home shortly they laugh.

"We don't mean to be hurtful, Faith, it's just that so many of us were told the same thing. When I came here I looked like you, nary a mark for the world to see," the woman who calls herself Lynette says to me. Her face is now scarred and deformed; I know her words aren't meant to sting, but they do. They are frightening and unsettling but I puff my chest and remain resolute. I am different. I will be the one to leave this place, I have to because my life waits outside the fence with my family and friends.

I decide to write my family at once. I brought stationery and a steel pen from home and address my first letter to Mother. I pour my heart out, begging her to do something to bring me home. I detail the devastation and leave nothing out, I want my mother to understand where she put me under lock and key. I sign the letter lovingly as Faith, and tell her I remain devout and hopeful. My letter to my sister is quite different; to Emily I admit my love for William and my longing for him. I enclose a letter to him and ask that she deliver it in secret. I tell Emily about the long walks I am taking to maintain my figure and describe the gardens, for if anything here possesses beauty it's the lush and bountiful gardens decorated and outlined with glass Coca Cola bottles turned upside down in the soil. I write my father and ask him to send money and goods that I can occupy myself with. I detest sewing, but will take it up along with crosstitch if I have to. I don't tell him that I plan to make a few accouterments for myself along with pillows and curtains for my home with William, but that is my intent.

Weeks pass by and I don't hear from home. I write everyone daily, postmarking the letters myself using the address of the P.O. box I was given. In another week my letters are all given back to me by the postmaster marked 'Returned to Sender'. Baffled and distraught I ask to make an appointment with Dr. Jo.

Dr. Jo speaks softly and kindly. His warm, capable hands take mine is his own. "Faith, it pains me deeply to see you in distress. I understand your family has not corresponded with you since your arrival?"

"No, they haven't. My letters have all been returned unopened and I can't understand why."

"It's customary for outgoing mail to be sterilized with hot steam before it is mailed, and because of this practice some recipients are fearful it has been tampered with. It's not the first time mail has gone unopened, but it is painful nonetheless."

"Have they forgotten about me already?"

"Forgotten, no, I doubt that. However, life does go on in the outside world. You are a bright, educated young woman, surely you know that."

"All too well I'm afraid."

"Time will tell, I encourage you to write once more and pray for a reply."

"I will do that, Dr. Jo, thank you."

"Faith, are you getting enough rest, your eyes have dark circles beneath them?" he asks.

"The nights are lonesome and I am not familiar with the sounds yet, but I do try, truly I do."

I leave the doctor's office and walk once more along the edge of the property, fondling the beads on my rosary that is always in my pocket. I have not been to the edge of the fence that overlooks the river yet and am determined to stretch my legs this afternoon. I go "home" and grab a peach from our kitchenette and proceed toward my destination. It's a lovely spring day, the birds are calling to one another and the smell of magnolias fills the air. I stop to smell the flowers and remind myself to be grateful, but am growing weary of having gratitude for so many unremarkable things, such as the perfectly browned toast complimented with just the right amount of butter, or the cleanliness and order to my cottage when I have heard others are not as well kept.

My peach is sweet and juicy. I walk along the meadows and see the fence in the distance. There even appears to be a tower for viewing the Mississippi River. Indeed! As I approach I see the levee has steps and patients are encouraged to take a gander at the boats and barges sailing on the river. I even hear a foghorn in the distance.

The sun's golden reflection rests gently upon the water and the brightly colored sails stir my soul and uplift me at once. I sigh with pleasure and sit on the wooden tower with crossed legs. This will be my special place, the place I come when I am down in the dumps. I can see fishermen along the water's edge and have a sudden urge to climb the fence and dangle my feet in the water. The women have told me what happens to those who try to escape and it's frightful. Apparently there is a detention center on campus and escapees serve time just like they would in the outside world. They are often brought back in shackles, turned in by their own families worried about the stigma of the disease and its effect on them.

I won't have to worry about that, I will get out of here in good health and be welcomed again by society. No one knows I am here, they are all jealous of the exploits I am said to be having in the grandest city of all, 'the Big Apple'.

I toss my peach pit towards the edge of the fence; perhaps it will grow a tree, perhaps not. I close my eyes and lay back on the well worn slats.

***

I must have fallen asleep because when I wake the sun is no longer high in the sky.

My spirits are uplifted and I am rejuvenated from the peaceful catnap. The sun always does wonders for my spirit too; mother never let me outdoors without a parasol, but I always preferred feeling the rays scorch my skin than shielding it. I have a dewy glow on my arms and my cheeks feel flushed as well.

I am in my room changing my clothing when I hear a knock on my door.

"You have a letter," Dorothy claims, handing me a manila envelope postmarked from an unknown address.

The letter is from Emily.

"Dearest Frances,

Mother and Daddy confided in me your true whereabouts so that I would stop pestering them about following you to New York. How dreadful for you! It has been almost a month since you have been gone and so much has changed. William has come to call for me in your absence. Mother approved and he and I are now going steady. He has plans to be a great lawyer one day, as I am sure you know. You mustn't be cross with me, dear sister, for both of us know that he had eyes for me all along. He is a darling suitor, bringing chocolates and flowers to impress our parents, no doubt. He stole a kiss from me two nights ago beneath a sky scattered with stars and it was as if we were the only two beings alive in that moment.

Mother is entangled in a bitter argument with Father over the household finances, but they both assure me nothing is seriously amiss. Mother is taking more wine with supper and even a glass or two of port by the fireplace after. Father works in his office most evenings and meets with his secretary now and then at odd hours for work-related problems.

Mother says you are not to write, she won't open any mail that has been tampered with. That is why I am writing you in secret, I have no return address for you I am afraid. You will be well enough soon and until then do say your prayers for those less fortunate.

Love,
Emily"

I crumple the letter from my calculating, bratty sister with shaky hands and crawl into bed before I lose my temper and punch something. I miss out on supper this evening and then skip breakfast in the morning. I have no wish to be disturbed.

My arms are heavy and my heart is filled with a slow burning feeling I can only acknowledge as hatred. My faith in the world is shattered. I feel betrayed and abandoned by those that are supposed to love me the most.

I feel more alone than ever before, it seems even God has abandoned me.

CHAPTER 6

ALONE

There is a funeral today for a patient who took his own life by drinking a bottle of Lysol. I don't condemn him or think he's going straight to hell like so many others do, instead I imagine the despair he must have felt that brought him to such a place. I prefer to rejoice that he is finally now at peace.

The man is buried in a small cemetery beside the pecan grove. There are rows of headstones lined with military precision on the well groomed grounds, few are engraved with details of the person who passed away. There are dozens of other patients that died before him and are buried here also. This man's headstone is also left unmarked to protect his family. Most people that die here nowadays remain at Carville. I was told that once several years ago after a small boy died, his body was boxed and shipped to his family as per their request. They only wanted to give him a proper burial on the land they loved. However, upon receiving the crate the family became quarantined and ostracized. Neighbors threatened to burn their house or shoot them if they didn't leave. They were forced to move away from their home and the son they buried in their pasture. Since then, when someone dies, families are notified and invited to attend the mass at Carville.

The Sisters of Charity do their best to stimulate us patients with activities and they provide love and encouragement in a variety of ways, yet there are only twenty-one of them and hundreds of us.

Despair is easy enough to come by in the outside world, but here inside Carville it's not a matter of why but when. It takes a very strong constitution to keep your chin up and spirit high. I have glimpsed that despair and even now feel its selfish hands take a hold of me and pull me under. I try to dust it off my shoulders but it's so difficult! Most days I allow it to wash over me and become my companion. I wallow and drown in self pity, focusing on everything that has been so cruelly taken from me. I dwell on all that I am missing at home, from my soft bed and delicious food, to the parties and dances.

If I didn't have a full schedule of appointments, I would not stray far from my bed today for I prefer to spend it sleeping. As it is now I have three pale patches of irritated skin as opposed to the one I had when I came here not so long ago. I still have a loss of sensation in the fingertips of my prominent hand but am learning to become ambidextrous so that I will always be able to write. The doctors need to check my progress since it's been a month that I have been on the vile chaulmoogra oil. The oil itself is foul smelling and hard to digest. It leaves me so nauseated that I can barely keep my food down, which is why I've lost so much weight.

"Faith, this is Dr. Murray, the Attending today. He specializes in pharmacology with a focus on chaulmoogra oil."

"Faith, I am pleased to meet you. How are you feeling on the oil, are you taking it as directed?"

"Quite honestly, I detest it. It leaves me feeling sick all day, just when my stomach starts to feel better it's time for another dose. Some patients call each pill "hope" but to me it's just vile."

"It appears you are having a local reaction to the shot as well. See, you are forming an abscess here. I will instruct the lab to titrate your injection dosage with olive oil and they will use your other arm for shots this week. I will also instruct them to mix two parts oil to one part lard to be applied to the rash directly three times daily. In the meantime, you need to soak the abscess twice daily in salt water to draw out the infection."

"Golly. I thought this was supposed to make me feel better, but all I feel is worse."

"I understand your concerns, but we've had great success with this treatment so far. If you continue to react, we will ask that you be admitted as a subject into our current trial for new medications. Currently we are testing potassium iodide, arsenic, and copper by way of injection. Some patients are having good results from the 'hot box' as well so we won't rule that out."

"Thank you, Dr. Murray," I say when I leave the office and walk towards the infirmary for my next appointment. I think about the courageous patients who are willing to subject themselves to experimentation, I suppose they are either heroic or hopeless and have nothing left to lose.

My next appointment is with Dr. Jo. He prescribes prolonged hot baths to draw out the disease both morning and night. He indicates that other patients are having success using hydrotherapy and light therapy, and if need be they could be added to my routine. Otherwise, I am told to continue to get my rest and take my medication. The doctor even suggests I borrow a bicycle and learn to ride, saying it would be good for my spirit. He inquires about my interests and reiterates that I might want to join one of the many clubs that have formed on campus. However, I am not interested in pottery or knitting and have no desire to learn how to make rugs or work with leather. I feel snooty that none of these appeal to me, but they don't.

It's plain to me that Dr. Jo understands that at this point my heart is more afflicted than my physical body. He promises to help in any way he can and offers me several books from his personal library to occupy my mind for the time being. I take the stack of books to be polite, although I have no intention to read them anytime soon. The only books I want to read are the bible and scientific journals with information about my disease, and those are difficult to come by.

I pass the ball fields on my way home but have no desire to

sit up high in the bleachers and watch the 'Carville Indians' scrimmage the 'Point Clair Indians', even though it looks like a lively crowd. I am not making friends here and as a result have become a loner of my own volition. Maybe that's not true, I do enjoy spending evenings chatting over snacks and tea with the ladies in my cottage. As long as we don't talk about things we miss from home it's okay.

Not only do I feel like an outcast here at times, but I also feel like a prisoner with no rights. We have no right to vote while we reside at the hospital nor are we allowed to use the telephones. We are not to mingle with the opposite sex except while chaperoned at dances and movies. Our cell-like rooms are inspected weekly and if anything is out of order, we are penalized.

When I get home tonight the ladies are chatting loudly and I overhear that a few Negroes are being sent home because they have tested negative for twelve consecutive months for leprosy. Oh please, God, let it be so. There is also talk of the schoolteacher being sent home. Hope tickles my throat and I laugh along with the women.

"Let's celebrate," one of the women says. She pulls out a bottle of whiskey and pours small glasses for everyone.

"There is a dance tonight, what do you say we all go and have a good time?"

"Here, here," everyone chimes and it is agreed we'll go as a unit. I've never liked whiskey but drink it down anyway. Its fiery taste burns my throat on the way down and warms my stomach instantly.

After supper my stomach is so upset that I heave three times. Although my oil is being tempered, it still affects me adversely. I have little to no energy and tell the women to go on without me. I can hear the band, comprised of musicians from the hospital, playing joyful tunes and I close my eyes and pretend I am there.

Hopefully by this time next season I will attend my own ball, find a new suitor, and start fresh. My eyes tear up at that but I refuse to shed them. If William can replace me with Emily so quickly he must not have really loved me as he indicated.

I curse my sister for stealing my boyfriend, and that's exactly what she did. I am sure she lured him to our house under false pretenses; all she had to do was bat her thick eyelashes and twirl her gorgeous blond hair and any man who wasn't blind would notice. She is a beauty, there is no denying that, and while I am more plain, I am certainly no louse.

I could spit nails I'm so angry. Just thinking of her betrayal combined with my parents' abandonment is enough to put me over the edge. Perhaps it would be better for everyone if I just slipped away and started a new life where no one knows me.

I carry my leaden body to the fence to stare out at the river, the moon's reflection paints a lovely picture and draws me in. If I could just get across the fence, I could run away and no one would have to worry about me.

CHAPTER 7

WATER

The evening is still and I sit alone on the levee listening to the sound of water rippling. I hear whispers and see a pair of lovers sneaking off to be together. Good for them, I think. In the outside world they would be chastised and berated, but in here no one would dare condemn true love. We are human beings with needs after all and love is the greatest cure for any affliction. The couple disappears and I am alone again. Suddenly, and much to my surprise, I see the lovebirds on the other side of the fence! How did they get there?

"You there?" I whisper.

The couple ducks and hides from sight, afraid of being caught.

"It's okay, I won't tell. I only want to know how you got across," I say into the darkness.

I climb down the watchtower and approach the fence. The couple comes towards me, their fingers entwined, eyes full of love and hunger.

"There is a hole underneath the fence, follow us and we'll show you," the man, named Bill, says to me.

I step lightly so I don't snap any branches and alert the guards.

"Here, just lift the bottom corner and crawl under," he says indicating where the hole is.

I do as I am told. The hole is not very deep so my clothes are dusty and my face is dirty when I crawl out.

"Thank you! It feels good to be on the other side of the fence for a change!" I say.

"Where will you go?" Janet, the woman, asks.

"I suppose I'll just walk along the edge for a while."

"I don't see why you can't tag along with us. We're going to the university to attend a party for a few hours, we just have to be back before the guards patrol the area."

"You don't say?" A party, how about that.

"We have friends there. They think we are students, but truthfully we just go so we can listen to music and dance together."

"That's very sweet, are you sure you won't mind if I tag along?"

"Not at all."

The three of us walk a half mile or so and are met by a cab where the path alongside the river meets the road. I don't have any money but Bill and Janet assure me they will pay the fee. The university is in Baton Rouge, not terribly far from my home. Panic overwhelms me when I realize I could be recognized!

"Stop the car, please turn around, Sir," I say to the driver.

"Faith, what's the matter?"

"I just don't think it's a good idea that I join you after all, but the two of you enjoy a dance or two for me," I say. Luckily we had only driven a mile or so toward the school.

I want so desperately to be normal and do normal activities that I was almost willing to risk it, but it is a gamble I can't take. If William or my sister got wind that I attended a school party it could destroy my entire family and even though I am mad at them right now, two wrongs don't make a right.

I find my way back to the hole in the fence but rather than crawl back through, I linger on the water's edge. I slip off my shoes and hold up my skirt while I wade into the swampy area. Mud oozes between my toes and my feet sink up to my ankles. The muscles in my shoulders relax and I feel the urge to swim. I swam regularly as a child when my father took us along for his fishing expeditions. Father even called me his 'little fish' because I took to the water so easily. One time he told me he was afraid I would start to grow gills if I didn't get out of the water.

I glance to my left and right to make sure I am truly alone, for what I am about to do is ludicrous. I lift my arms and pull my shirt off over my head. I step out of my skirt and put the articles of clothing in a pile beside a rock. I leave my brassiere and underpants on and slip into the water until it covers my shoulders and I feel free at last.

Submerged. Unencumbered. Alive.

JENNY

CHAPTER 8

NUMBNESS

"You're bleeding. Nanny nanny boo boo," my older sister Sally taunts. She poked me with her stick on purpose while we were playing outdoors. She is cruel, especially when we're out of Mama's sight. She teases me something awful; calling me bad names like 'baby' and 'dummy'. She is the meanest big sister in the world and I hate her. I know I am not supposed to hate, but I do.

I don't feel any pain but when I look at my knee I see a wound with blood trickling out of it. I wonder why I don't feel anything?

"Mama, I'm bleeding," I call to my mother when we come running in from the woods.

"Come here, Jenny. I'll take care of it," Mama is tired but greets me with open arms. Five sons and two daughters under the age of thirteen keep Mama busy.

"It's deep, what happened? Did you trip again?" Mama asks because I'm known for being clumsy.

"It was Sally, she poked me," I say.

"I did not," Sally stands before us with her hands placed defiantly on her hips. "Besides, she didn't feel it anyway until I told her she was bleeding. I think she fell, Mama."

"What do you mean you didn't feel it?" Mama asks with a look of concern that causes a crease between her eyebrows.

"It doesn't hurt is all," I say shrugging my shoulders.

"It doesn't smart? Well, it's deep enough that I should stitch it together. I should take you into town to see the doctor but we simply can't afford it and my needle is as good as any."

"Sally, fetch me my sewing kit."

"Now, Jenny, don't worry. I'll be done before you can say,

'Bob's your uncle', or sing your ABCs."

Mama threads and knots her smallest needle and tells me to hold my breath and count to three. On three she punctures the skin fold and pulls the thread through the hole. She pokes the skin on the other side and then pulls once more and knots it together.

"Are you okay, darling girl?"

"It doesn't smart, Mama. I don't feel a thing," I say again feeling proud of my bravery.

"My goodness, you are strong-willed."

Mama continues to stitch me up, poking holes, and pulling the thread taught until I have a total of nine stitches in my leg. She rewards me with a cold glass of sweet tea and two sugar cookies and snuggles me on her lap for a few minutes before one of the young-uns gets into trouble and she's pulled away. Sally gives me a dirty look and I know she wishes she didn't hurt me now.

"Miss Miller says if we don't feel a spot on our skin we need to report it because it could mean we have a disease," she adds.

"Does not," I say.

"Does too, I'm telling Mama."

Sally tells Mama what Miss Miller said and instead of brushing it aside and ignoring Sally, Mama comes at me with her needle again.

"Jenny, I'm just going to poke around your knee a little. Tell me if you feel anything." Mama puts my leg across her lap and pokes lightly at my wound. When I can't feel the slightest prick she jabs the needle deeper.

"Ouch," I say when she reaches higher up my leg.

"It does appear to be a numb patch. Dear me. We better keep you in the loft for now, at least until your daddy comes home. Run along," she says.

"But why? I want to play with the boys."

"Jenny, do as your told. Go on up to the loft and write me a story, use your imagination and we'll read it together this evening."

"Okay, Mama."

I climb the ladder to the loft I share with my sister. I lay on my belly and stretch across the bed, letting my arms dangle over the mattress, fingertips brushing the wide plank wooden floorboards. I flip over onto my backside and stare at the ceiling thinking about my story. I am in the fourth grade at school and the teacher says I have a vivid imagination considering I am only ten years old. I pull my knee up and uncover the bandage Mama placed across the wound to keep the blood in. I press the wound and blood oozes out, a few stitches almost come unraveled too. I don't feel anything. I am brave. I am the bravest girl in the world, and I'll write a story about that.

"Once upon a time, there was a girl named Jennifer, but everyone called her Jenny," I start. I must have fallen asleep because when I wake up I can hear Daddy and Mama talking about me in hushed voices.

"She can't go to school, we'll keep her here with us so no one finds out," Daddy says.

"What about the others? What if we all catch it?" Mama asks.

"We won't, if we keep her in the loft, or outside, we'll be fine," Daddy's voice sounds funny.

"What if Sally tells the teacher? She'll be taken from us or worse," Mama worries.

"People are afraid, Jane, it will be a blight on our family. There is a mandatory quarantine for anyone with leprosy. We could move; I can get work a few towns over, Baton Rouge or New Orleans."

"We can't be sure it's leprosy, Jim. But if it is people will find out, even if we move deeper in the country," Mama cries.

"Not if we hide her well enough. We'll keep her busy indoors, she can help you with the chores."

"I don't know, Jim. We have to consider the others."

"We could take her to Carville, she'll be close enough to visit…" Daddy says.

"Oh, Jim, I couldn't, it wouldn't be right. She would be all alone there."

"I know, Jane. I know. It's just a thought. Let's sleep on it tonight. For now she'll stay in the loft until we figure out what to do."

Sally was put to bed on the davenport and the boys were nestled in the room all four of them shared. Baby Joey, the youngest among us, is only nine months old so he sleeps in a bassinet beside Mama. He still nurses and Mama doesn't want him to wake all of us at night with his cries.

Usually in the mornings I occupy the four year old twins, Danny and Michael, while Mama tends to Joey and the meals with Sally's help. Nolan, my seven year old brother, plays with us too. My oldest brother, Sam, is thirteen and he helps Daddy around the house with manly chores like chopping firewood and feeding the animals. When I wake up this day Mama tells me I can come down to use the bathroom and grab a bowl of oatmeal but then I have to take it back upstairs. Sally plays with the twins and Nolan helps Mama with Joey.

"Mama, why? Is it the numb patch? Does it mean I have a disease like Sissy said?" I ask.

"It could, and we need to be safe is all. Daddy and I are figuring out what to do, don't you worry," Mama assures me with a sweet smile.

"Are we going to have to move?" I ask.

"Were you eavesdropping, Jenny? You know that's not polite. I don't have the answers yet, but as I said we'll figure something out."

"Mama, I don't want to move," Sally interjects. "Just because she's sick, doesn't mean we all have to suffer. It's not fair," she pouts as she stomps and creates a fuss.

"I'm not sick!" I shout and storm my way from the bathroom back up to the loft. I pick up the hairbrush and count one hundred strokes. I braid my hair and twist it into a comely bun. I put on a dress and tie up my leather shoes. "Hmph. I am not sick," I say to myself.

The hours tick by and Mama entertains me from her place in the kitchen below. She instructs me to repeat my times tables loud enough so that she can hear. When we are done with that she instructs me to read, then to practice my penmanship. It's what I would be doing in school, but I am itching to come down from the loft and go outside.

"Mama, can I go outside for a while?" I plead.

"Alright, but stay out of the garden, there's a bee hive as large as a watermelon that Daddy needs to move. Don't wander too far," she calls after me.

I climb a few trees and try to fall and hurt myself on purpose. When I scrape my elbow it smarts alright, I hold back tears because it stings and bleeds. Tiny pebbles and flecks of dirt are stuck to my skin and I attempt to clean the cut myself. I can't clean it out thoroughly so I head home to get Mama's help.

When I arrive home I notice two unfamiliar men speaking with Mama on our front porch. They are wearing professional looking suits and ties, and one even has a top hat. Their black Ford is parked in our dirt driveway. I hide from sight and do my best to hear what the strangers are saying.

"Ma'am, we just want to evaluate the child, we mean her no harm," the taller of the two men says.

I don't know what evaluate means. The second man tells Mama

he wants to check all the children in the house and determine whether or not we need to be in quarantine. That's another word I am not entirely certain of but I think it means locked up.

"Please come back when my husband is home. Until then, I have children to take care of. Good day," Mama says, moving away from the men and back inside, shutting the screen door behind her.

I watch the men stroll down our driveway and get into their car.

"Mama, what did they want?" I ask sneaking up behind her as she mixes butter and flour into dough for biscuits.

"Jenny, sit down. The men are worried you may have a disease. Now I know you are a good child, but some say the disease is sent to those who are sinners. You haven't done any sinning now have you?"

"No ma'am. I sure haven't." I think hard about my activities over the course of the last few weeks but nothing bad comes to mind. That's not entirely true, I have allowed hatred to creep into my heart, but I asked the Father for forgiveness during my confession and said my rosary for absolution.

"I believe you, you are too sweet for your own good. Your father will be home shortly and he and I will discuss this then. Until then, take some ham and cheese and head up to the loft." I cut myself a slice of hard cheese and wrap it in a thick slice of maple ham. It's delicious.

Daddy comes through our front door an hour or so later and asks mama what happened. The men paid him a visit at work and told him she had been most uncooperative.

"Pack up the house, we'll take what we can and leave tonight," he orders.

"Jim, are you absolutely certain? Is there another way?" Mama asks Daddy.

"Not unless you want to take her to Carville, even then we may be put in quarantine. The Johnson's have a big 'X' scratched across their door and we'll be next if we wait one second longer."

"Jenny? Pack your things, put your clothes in your pillowcase and do the same for Sally. We'll be moving on today and need to be ready when she and Sam get home from school," Mama instructs.

I strip our bedsheets and use them to carry anything I can't fit in our pillowcases. I empty our drawers and am extra careful with our breakables. I hear someone knocking on our door and look down over the loft. The men are back and this time they barge into our home and demand to see me. Mama is teary eyed and Daddy stands in their way. They threaten to have Daddy arrested and I can't stand to be the cause of trouble any longer.

"I'm here. I'll come down."

"Jenny? I'm Dr. Richter. I'd like to examine you, if I may. The school reported you were absent today and your sister said you weren't feeling well, that you had a numb patch. May I see it, please?"

I lift my dress up over my kneecap and roll down my stockings. The doctor puts on his specs and examines my wound. He gently pokes and prods the area with different tools, none of which I am able to feel, not even the sharp edged blade. When he uses the same tools on my other leg. I yelp in pain.

"Folks, it appears the child has leprosy. I'll need to examine everyone in the house at once."

Mama goes first, the doctor pokes and prods her skin, he checks her for moles and lesions and declares her healthy. My daddy is healthy too, and so are Nolan and Michael. When it's time for Danny's examination my mama hesitates. I notice that she's chewing the inside of her cheek and fidgeting an awful lot with her hands. When the doctor rolls up Danny's shirt we see an angry rash spreading out from his belly button. The doctor turns Danny on his belly and checks his back, he says he is looking for more bumps, pale colored moles, or signs of muscle weakness to determine the severity of his case.

"How long?" the doctor asks Mama.

"A few months. I noticed it over the winter, he's the only one."

"There are two other children who reside here, correct?"

"Yes, Sir. They're at school. You may wait if you'd like."

Mama makes tea for the doctor. He is a kind man with a hard job to do; even I know that.

The door opens and Sam and Sally walk in. Sally's jaw drops and she slumps over. "I'm sorry, Mama. It's my fault."

"What's your fault, Dear?"

"I told them Jenny had a mark, they asked and I told them. I'm sorry."

"There, there, it's alright. We should never lie and you did as you were told. The doctor needs to examine you and Sam so please drop your belongings and let's get it over with." After thorough examinations, Sam and Sally are both given clean bills of health.

"You'll be under strict quarantine, folks. We'll mark your household accordingly and no one will be allowed to leave. You may not accept visitors either."

"Do we have to take them to Carville? Can't they stay here with us a while longer?" Mama asks the doctor.

"I am afraid the law states anyone in Louisiana with leprosy must be admitted, by force if necessary, to the hospital at once. I'm sorry folks, these aren't my rules, but guidelines established by the town leaders."

"How will they treat it?"

"I'm afraid I can't answer that…I suppose lots of rest and proper nourishment. There is a team of five doctors there that has a better understanding of the disease than I do. I'm terribly sorry about this, good day." The doctor tips his hat and leaves.

Sally is hysterical, and Sam is confused. Mama and Daddy talk in private in their bedroom.

"Children, we are going to load up the car and leave tonight, everyone pitch in and we'll be on our way before supper."

"Daddy, no!" Sally interrupts. "They're sick and we'll just have to keep moving. Can't we leave 'em here? I told Jenny to wash better, but she wouldn't listen and now she is a dirty leper!"

"Sally! Mind your tongue. We will not leave your siblings behind. You should be ashamed of yourself, now apologize," my daddy says.

"I won't," Sally says, running outdoors as far away from me as possible.

"What about Carville?" Mama asks.

"What's Carville, Daddy?" I want to know.

"Carville is a place, a hospital, not far from here, where people like you and Danny live. They have nuns who take care of the patients, and doctors too. We may not have a choice, I'm afraid."

"Is it settled then?" Mama asks through tears.

"I suppose it's for the best. We'll head towards Carville tonight and move on from there." Daddy can't look at me, he stares at the ground and kicks the floor with his worn steel toed boot.

CHAPTER 9

CARVILLE

We load the car with all of our belongings and leave our house before supper time. I settle Danny on my lap and Mama situates herself between me and the others. She hands out biscuits and cheese, apples and ham slices for our meal. Everyone is quiet.

"You must be brave and take care of Danny. Can you do that?" she whispers to me so the others don't hear.

"Will I see you again, Mama?" I'm trying not to cry but my heart aches and I don't know what I did wrong. I am not dirty, I bathe as much as the others and always wash behind my ears.

"I'll visit as often as I can. I'll write you as well, we can even be pen pals. There will be a school there and I expect you to remain on top of your studies and to be a good girl and stay out of trouble."

"I promise, Mama," I gulp, swallowing my tears.

The dirt road is long and winding. Moss covered oak trees line it on both sides, providing shade and beauty. There is a pecan orchard and a lake and I can see gardens in the distance even though the sun is behind the clouds and the day is turning to dusk. Up ahead I see buildings through a tall fence. Daddy slows the vehicle and opens the car door. Danny and I say goodbye to our siblings from a distance and Mama and Daddy lovingly take our hands and walk us to a big locked gate. Daddy rings the bell next to the gate and we wait for someone to respond.

Mama pauses as we approach the grounds, "Jenny, I think it would be wise if you use your middle name, Diane, from now on. Danny will use his as well, so from now on the two of you are Diane and Gregory Wilson. You can use my maiden name for your surname so you always have a piece of me," Mama says, bestowing me with one last gift.

"Why, Mama? Why do I have to change my name, what did I do wrong?" I begin to weep.

"Think of your new name as a fresh start, for all of us. You did nothing wrong. Now be a brave girl," Mama whispers as I cling to her skirt.

A woman wearing a white robe and white, stiff, winged hat approaches us. She unlocks the gate and introduces herself as Sister Anne. She promises my parents that she will personally watch over the two of us. Danny sucks his thumb while I bite my nails, uncertain of this Sister person as well as what waits for us behind the fence.

The sign reads: U.S. Marine Hospital #66.

The sister reaches for my hand but I cling tighter to Mama. I circle her leg with my arms and lock my hands together tightly. Daddy wiggles my fingers apart releasing me from Mama. He doesn't hug me or Danny, he simply turns his back and walks away with his head slung low, afraid to show his tears. Mama covers her mouth with both hands to muffle her cries, she reaches out to us, but Sister Anne is already directing us away to the other side of the fence. Danny thinks he is on a grand adventure, but I know the truth, we may never see Mama or the rest of our family again.

CHAPTER 10

DANNY

Sister Anne walks my brother and me through a lengthy corridor that leads to a dining hall.

"Would you like a bed-time snack, children? We have ice cream, chocolate or vanilla, or maybe a little scoop of each?" the Sister asks.

Danny nods his head 'yes' but I remain quiet. Sister leaves momentarily while she dishes up the ice cream. Danny and I sit together at a table and wait.

"Here you are, my darlings. When you are finished we will check you into your rooms."

"Sister, Mama wants me to stay with my brother."

"Of course, Dear. Normally the men and women are separated, but in this case we will allow it. Danny, or should I say, Gregory, will stay with you in your room until he is a little bit older."

"Are there other children?" I ask, noting how quiet and spare it is here.

"Why yes, of course. Sister Josephine and I take care of the children, we have regular school days and lots of play time. I think you'll enjoy yourself here."

"I'm in the fourth grade," I say.

"Very good, you will fit in with our older elementary students then. Danny will start to learn his letters with the pre-school group and he'll have lots of time to play outdoors and enjoy the fresh air."

"Where is everyone?" I ask.

"I suspect most of the patients are at evening mass. I'll expect you to attend the morning mass, and I will give you a tour of the facility then as well. Now let's show you to your room and get you both settled for the night."

Sister Anne holds our hands and directs us to a wing adjacent to the building designed to house the children. Our room is mostly bare except for two beds with gray sheets and handknit blankets in bright colors spread across them.

Although there are two beds, Danny cuddles up beside me and sucks his thumb. He is my responsibility now and I won't let anything happen to him. I stroke his hair and sing him to sleep with a lullaby, when I hear his steady breathing I stop singing. I listen to the unfamiliar sounds around me, aside from a child fussing somewhere down the hall everything is quiet. I vow not to be afraid. I vow to keep my chin up and carry on as Mama would want me to, but in the morning when I wake and a new day starts, I am scared to death.

"Up you go, Danny. Time to get ready for breakfast," I say unable to refer to him as Gregory.

I wet my fingertips and smooth out his hair before tending my own. My clothing has not arrived nor has Danny's so we wear the outfits we slept in even though they are wrinkled. Sister Anne greets us with warm welcoming hugs and a kiss to the forehead.

"How did you sleep?" she asks.

"Fine, Sister," I say bluffing.

"Follow me then, we'll go to the dining hall first and then on to mass."

I can't possibly count all the folks in the dining hall this morning, but every chair and table is full to the brim with people talking, eating, and reading newspapers. A few folks look our way, but I shield my eyes from the horror. Danny cries and clings to my legs, I pick him up and he settles his head onto my shoulders. I pass a man without lips, his face is riddled with lesions and his hands are missing fingers. He reaches out to us, but I walk quickly past.

"No need to be afraid, Diane, they are just people, like you."

Sister Anne seats us with a group of children but I have no appetite. When the toast arrives I push it aside. I can't even drink the milk that is offered. Danny sips orange juice and nibbles an apple and I am grateful that he is able to maintain his appetite in the face of such despair.

Everywhere I dare to look I see horrible, scary faces and people that are disabled. People have missing limbs and use wheelchairs to get around. Arms and legs are wrapped in bandages and some folks have purple mud smeared across their faces. I don't want to be here. Everywhere I look I see people dressed in rags with open sores and gaping wounds. It's scares me and I start to cry.

"Sister, I don't want to be here," I say through my tears.

"There, there, let's take a walk outside," Danny and I follow her lead and walk across wooden boards towards the Catholic church. As we enter the house of God I hear sweet voices and see what appears to be angels standing on the altar.

"The Sisters have formed a choir, they sound lovely, have a listen."

The Sisters of Charity wear white robes and white winged caps that make them look like angels. I close my eyes and listen to the music, allowing it to fill my soul and give me courage. Danny and I sit in the first pew of the church and wait for the priest to begin the mass. I notice there are two separate chalices for communion. One chalice is for the staff and the other for the patients. I have never seen such a thing and decide to ask Sister Anne about it later.

The priest speaks of loving thy neighbor and having an open heart. He says we must be willing to give and receive our Lord's love and pay it forward and I believe he is talking directly to me.

"We may ask ourselves, Why me?" he preaches, "I ask why not you? Perhaps our Lord has chosen you to be here among the humble, crippled souls, to learn what it truly means to abide the commandments. Perhaps it is your abiding faith and your love that will make the difference here at Carville. We are not alone, we have each other, we have love to give and receive."

I stiffen up, knowing full well I did not treat the folks I encountered this morning with kindness. Instead I turned my back on nearly every poor soul I saw. I could not look at the suffering, not just out of fear but because I don't want to be like them.

I listen carefully to the Father's words and promise to try harder. I begin by hugging Danny and smiling brightly so he knows he has me. When church is over Sister Anne takes the two of us to visit with the doctor.

"Well, hello there, children. What are your names?"

"I am Diane and this is Gregory," I stammer, the names feeling uncomfortable and unfamiliar.

"Very well. Diane, let's have a look, shall we?" he asks.

The doctor examines my knee and makes notations in his notebook. He spends far more time with my brother because his rash is blistering and forming lesions.

Danny is treated with a purple ointment and I am told to bring him again tomorrow morning after mass. The ointment is to help the burning sensation and keep the lesions from spreading.

We walk back through the long, covered corridor past the dining hall and dormitories to what appears to be a classroom for school. There are rows of books and a chalkboard in the front of the room. Danny goes with Sister Anne to a room for smaller children while I remain here.

"Diane, it is nice to have you with us, we are just about to work on our cursive. Please grab a slate and I'll be around in a moment."

Some of the children look my way, some even smile. I count

nine boys and six girls in my class. When our lesson is over we are released for recess in the surrounding yard. I see the fence; it's twelve feet high and has three lines of barbed wire on the top.

"It's so you can't escape," a girl says to me. "My name's Dorothy, what's yours?" she asks. I nearly say Jenny, but remember I am now Diane.

I am baffled we are fenced in, is it that bad in here?

"People still try to escape, especially the men. There is a hole below the fence over yonder, the men sneak out in the evening after supper and go to the Louisiana State football games, they come back good and drunk lots of times. Once or twice they've come back shackled, and get a scolding, but most of 'em would do it again just to get out of here and see a game. The rest of us just play games here. Some people golf and others play tennis. We even have a softball team. There's a game this afternoon at the fields, you should come and sit with me in the bleachers. Sister makes boiled peanuts and everyone has a jolly good time."

"Swell. I've never seen a game, I suppose it would be fun."

"We also have choir and Sister Theresa teaches piano lessons. There is a doll house in the playroom, have you seen it yet?"

"No," I gulp. "I don't have any dolls to play with," I admit. My family was not well off and rarely did we have such extraordinary, impractical gifts.

"You can share mine," Dorothy says grabbing my hand and skipping away with me.

The doll house has two stories; on the ground level there is a kitchen, dining room, living room, and grand foyer. The stairs lead to four bedrooms and a center hall bathroom. In place of real dolls children have modeled wooden clothes pins or sticks and pecan shells to craft people. Beds are made from left over scraps of material and some even have their own handknit blankets. It's lovely and I am delighted because I have never played with anything like this before.

When three girls come towards the house to play I back away, knowing I have to share. Everyone is friendly, the girls ask me to join and we have a good time playing at family. The mother makes supper and the daddy works in the yard while the children take naps and play games.

Sister Catherine brings Danny to me in the middle of our fun because he is inconsolable. "Mama," he keeps repeating over and over. He misses Mama and it hasn't even been one full day. The rash on his belly looks fierce and I can tell he's been scratching it all morning long. His eyes are watery and puffy too.

The doctor coats his belly once again with the purple ointment and covers it with a thick bandage. He examines his eyes and has him take a vision test. Danny doesn't know his letters so he asks me to stand six feet away and hold up objects that should be familiar to him. The doctor asks Danny to describe what he sees but it's a difficult task and he is unable to do it.

"We'll continue to observe his eyesight, if you notice him bumping into things or having difficulty of any kind let me know," the doctor says.

"Surely, I will. Doctor, when will Danny, I mean, Gregory, and I get to go home?"

"Carville is your home now, and we are all your family."

CHAPTER II

DOROTHY

This morning when I wake up I find a pink slip that has been slid under my door sometime during the night. It's a notice that I have a letter waiting for me at the post office. I run across the grounds to the Carville post office and rip the envelope open at once. I can hardly sit still to read it because I am so excited to hear from home.

"Dearest Diane,

   Your father, siblings, and I hope you and Gregory are doing well. We miss you something awful but know you are in a good place with kind people. I hope you have made friends and are enjoying your studies.

   We have moved to a new town that is satisfactory for now. There are pecans growing right in our very own yard. I've put the pots and pans away and made up all the beds. For the time being it is home sweet home.

   We're keeping a close eye on your sister and brothers to see if they develop any symptoms of leprosy like you and your brother. So far everyone is healthy.

   I am knitting you a shawl, and will make your brother a sweater. Please hug him for me and tell him I love him.

                                                        All my love,
                                                        Mama

   I re-read Mama's letter over and over. If she knew how badly Danny wanted her she would come for him at once.

   "The letters are sterilized, ya know," my best friend Dorothy tells me.

"Jeepers, is that so?" I ask wondering why.

"All the mail is steamed before it comes in or goes out. It's just one of the rules, I reckon."

"There sure are a lot of rules here. I wish I could just go home," I admit.

"At least you got a letter, I've been here for four years and never had one."

"I'm sorry, Dorothy. Why that's horrible. Do you think our families just forget about us?"

"Maybe. It's best if we make do. It's pretty here, and we have each other."

"It is pretty, you're right. I've never seen the lake, though, can you show me?"

On our way towards the lake we see a man arriving in chains. An officer escorts him against his will to the administration building. The man has patches across his face and welts on his wrists and knees, he looks like the living dead and I say so to Dorothy.

"Poor fellow," she musters. "It happens often, people brought here from pest houses or hospitals by sealed box car or crate or, as you just saw, in chains. They'll search him for guns and knives before they let him loose, don't worry. It ain't so bad here, you'll see. First one to the lake look-out is the winner!

We run towards a perch that allows us to see the boats sailing along the Mississippi River. Patients picnic along the fence; the men and woman aren't allowed to interact, but here, away from the watchful eyes of the staff they do. Some spread blankets or quilts and just lounge in the sun, while others are more brazen and cuddle. What I wouldn't give to swim, the prickly heat is causing me to sweat under my sundress and I need to cool down. Swimming is in my blood, Mama told me many times. I am like a fish that could stay under water longer than any of my siblings.

Yet the waterway is on the other side of the fence and I wouldn't want to risk crawling through the hole for a swim.

"Let's go back, there is going to be a movie tonight and I have to write a letter and check in on my brother," I say turning my grief towards brighter things.

"Okay, race ya!"

Dorothy and I run and skip through the fields, she's far ahead of me and I try to catch up and resort to a gallop. Up ahead I see my friend and she appears to be slowing down.

"I'm going to beat you!" I say passing her. I happen to glance down and see blood on her right foot, we are barefoot and that is our first mistake.

"Dorothy, your foot."

"I guess I better go see the doctor."

"Does it hurt? Here, hold on to my shoulder and we'll go together."

"I can't feel it so I'm okay walking."

We arrive at the infirmary and while Dorothy is having her foot taken care of I check on Danny. I know his name is Gregory now but I just can't think of him that way.

"Sissy," he says putting his arms up in the air towards me. I lift him and hug him tight.

"Would you like to rock a bit?"

Danny nods 'yes', so we get comfortable in a rocking chair on the sunporch. Danny's eyes are swollen and red. They must itch because he rubs them as much if not more than his belly. His belly has dried blood from all his scratching and I remember that Mama used to put a soothing cool rag on our skin when we had poison ivy. I leave him in the chair for a bit and collect a cool cloth, I soothe his angry skin and sing him a lullaby. My poor baby brother certainly could never have done anything bad enough to deserve this, so perhaps it isn't from sinning after all.

"Mama?" Danny asks.

"Shhh," I say, leaning his head against my chest while we rock.

***

Room inspections are this evening before the movie. I make my bed and fold my blanket and take care of Danny's as well. I check my clothing to be sure it's clean and presentable. I pick up the spare sock lying on the ground and fluff our pillows. I empty our garbage can and wait. Sure enough my room is satisfactory and I am granted a movie pass.

The movies are shown in the old dining hall. It's quite dingy in here but at least we get to enjoy an entertaining film. There is a hole in the wall called 'The Canteen' that serves soft drinks and candy! I don't have any money but Dorothy shares her snacks with me and we sit next to each other to enjoy the show. Dorothy's foot is bandaged tight but blood seeps through the material and I know it will need a new dressing before bed. Sister Anne explained to me that some of the folks lose feeling in their extremities and don't realize when they get hurt. Infections take over the wound and that's when folks lose their fingers and limbs. I know about not having feeling because that happened to my leg when I fell in the woods.

"Do they just fall off, sister?" I ask.

"No, they reabsorb into the body, it's complicated I know," she answers honestly.

It's dreadful and frightening and I hope it doesn't happen to Dorothy. She said the disease also affects the mucous membranes which is why so many patients here have holes where their noses and lips used to be.

My mind is full of scary images, but at least we go to bed with full bellies. Danny cuddles up with me on the single mattress we share and he scratches himself all night. In the morning I take him to see the doctor and we discover his rash has spread like wildfire. It looks awful and has to feel like pins and needles.

Danny whines and fusses and it's hard to take his mind off his ailment. I even try reading to him but he can't make out the pictures through the slits in his swollen eyes.

"His eyes are infected. Many of the patients here are blind, it's one of the symptoms of leprosy. Your brother has a very aggressive case and we'll do everything we can to keep him comfortable."

"Thank you, Doctor. What can I do?"

"If the cool cloth helped, you can keep applying that. Leave the rest to the Sisters, they will take care of him while you're in school. It's important to keep on top of your studies, young lady, then maybe you can help in the infirmary one day."

"Hmm." I'd never thought of that, but I do reckon I would like making people more comfortable.

CHAPTER 12

VISIT FROM HOME

Sister Anne has exciting news; today our mother is coming to visit. The Sister walks with me to the fence and instructs me to wait for my mama who will be along shortly. I cling to the chain link and wait patiently for Mama but when I see her walking in my direction, I run as fast as my legs allow.

"Mama!"

"Jenny, I mean Diane, where is Danny?"

"He isn't well enough to be here, Mama. I'm trying my best but his eyes are swollen and he can't see very well. His rash is spreading, he scratches it all night long and he wants you…"

"I'm sure he does, but I am grateful he has you. You're a good big sister," Mama says blinking back tears, trying to hide her pain.

"Can't you come in? You could make him all better, I know it."

"I can't, your father won't allow it. I'd be putting the family in jeopardy, I'm sorry."

Mama looks worn out and I don't know who is more sad, me or her. We lock fingers through the fence and share a meal of cold chicken and cheese, dried apricots and sweetbread with honey glaze. She quizzes me on my sums and letters, and sits with me for two hours before I have to get ready for mass.

"You look good. I'm sorry you're in here on your own. We all love you, especially your daddy, it's just too hard for him to see you and Danny locked up like this."

"Tell Daddy that the food is good here, we have chicken and gravy with biscuits, or ham and beans with corn fritters. Every week there is a movie and on movie night we get to eat ice cream and cake. There is even a canteen at the theater and if we have money we can buy soft drinks and snacks."

"You always make the best of everything. I definitely think it's your greatest attribute. Now hug your brother for me and tell him that I love him," she hands me a brown bag full of peaches to share and then reaches into her purse and hands me what little change she has so I can use it at the Canteen. Then she leaves me again.

"Mama!" I sob and she turns to wave.

The visit leaves me feeling sad and blue. I miss my family and my old home and seeing Mama only makes me more homesick.

***

Danny's health is dwindling and I am afraid to leave his side for even one minute. I do my schoolwork at his bedside and eat my meals in our room.

In the morning I notice his open wounds cover most of his body and they appear to be festering. His eyes are rolled up into his head and he struggles to breathe.

"Sister!" I yell.

Sister Anne finds me holding my lifeless brother. His last breath was peaceful and I know his suffering has ended. Why then is it so hard for me to hand him over?

"We will give him a proper and loving burial, he deserves that much."

There are several rows of graves on the far side of the property and my brother will be laid to rest there.

The director tries his best to locate my family so that they can attend the funeral, but after a few days with no success we have to tend the corpse of my brother. My heart sinks and I feel sad and angry. Not even the birds singing or my best friend can pull me from the depths of my sadness.

Why should I behave if we are all going to die here anyway? I decide at this moment to run away.

CHAPTER 13

FINDING FAITH

I am supposed to be in class at the moment but because of my brother's death a few days ago, the teachers have given me a few days off to mourn. I use the time to pack a change of clothes and hide them under my bed. Inspections were yesterday so no one will find them today. I join Dorothy at dinner and am happy that chicken fricassee is on the menu because it's my favorite meal here. I slop up the gravy with my biscuits and eat every bite on my plate. I even grab an extra biscuit to pack in my pillowcase and take with me. After I eat, I sneak down to the water's edge and try desperately to find the hole under the fence. I am determined to get away, but a pair of hands grab me from behind.

"Just what do you think you're doing? Hmm?" A young woman places her hands on my shoulders, preventing me from going any further.

"I am running away," I declare, unwavering.

"You won't get very far I'm afraid," the lady says. "There are guards stationed all around the property now, dear. They'll bring you back in cuffs and put you in the clink if you aren't careful."

"I am going to swim across the river," I say standing my ground.

"That's a mighty long swim, and the water is chilly at night."

"It doesn't matter. I am a strong swimmer, I can make it."

"You could drown, or get hit by a barge. I suppose if you're going to swim for it I'll have to join you," the lady says kicking off her shoes.

I drop my bag in defeat, it's nothing but wishful thinking that I can run away from this place, this prison.

"My name is Faith, what's yours?"

"My real name is Jenny, but everyone here calls me Diane."

Faith spreads a blanket on the cool ground and invites me sit beside her and watch the sun set over the Mississippi River.

"I'd love to help you if you need a friend."

"I already have a friend," I say.

"What's her name?"

"Dorothy."

"Does Dorothy know you plan to escape tonight? I bet if she did she wouldn't allow it."

"She wouldn't, that's why I didn't tell her." I feel tears sting my eyes and suddenly the loss of my brother overwhelms me.

"Oh, honey, tell me what's wrong," the lady says.

"My brother died two days ago, my mama doesn't even know yet. They buried him already and now I am afraid she'll be mad," I admit.

"There, there. Why on earth would your mother be mad at you?"

"Because I let him die, I tried to take care of him, but he just got worse and worse," tears spill from my eyes and snot runs down my nose. I wipe it on my wrist and then on the grass.

"Would you like to go see his grave and say a special prayer?" the lady asks.

"I'd like that," I admit.

Faith folds her wool blanket and reaches for my hand. We walk across the property until we are at the pecan orchard where the cemetery is. A mound of freshly dug soil is three rows back, and beside it is the hole that Danny was buried in yesterday. Now another poor soul waits for his funeral tomorrow. Somehow knowing souls are all around my brother helps.

"Jenny? Shall I call you Jenny in secret?"

"Yes," I whisper, not wanting to part with my real name.

"Jenny, I am sure Danny knows how much you loved him. It's

not your fault he died. Just like it's not your fault you're in here. We have a disease that scares people, it's true, but we didn't do anything bad to deserve it. Maybe God put us in here because he has a plan for us? You know he would never give us more than we could handle. Perhaps we were even meant to find each other to help one another get through the hard times?"

Faith squeezes my hand and suddenly I don't feel so lonely anymore. We say a few words over Danny's grave and Faith takes me to her cottage. She makes me a cup of tea using her own electric hotplate to boil water. She adds extra sugar to my chipped cup and the chamomile tastes deliciously like home.

When we finish our drinks, she walks me back to my dorm where I'll now be sleeping in a room alone. I hesitate to go in but Faith promises she'll be by in the morning to visit.

My sheets smell like Danny. His blanky is more worn than mine and I hold it between my fingers and rub the soft fraying edges. I think of my baby brother and pray over his soul. I think about my family too and pray they know I did my best.

FAITH

CHAPTER 14

FINDING GRACE

During today's mass Father reminds us that, "Grace meets us where we are."

Truer words were never spoken. I recognize it here at Carville in the genuine kindness and compassion the Sisters bestow on all of us patients. I feel it in their loving caresses and heartfelt smiles. I find it in the good nature of the children who share what little they have with one another. I hear it in their laughter and read about it in the "Star 66" newspaper.

It took me the better part of six months to understand grace and even longer to accept it and come to terms with my misfortune. Choosing to be present in the moment has been my greatest obstacle, but now I think I have finally managed to put the past where it belongs, behind me.

I have been away from home for almost a year to the day with no correspondence from anyone except the boastful letter from Emily in my first lonely weeks. I no longer write my family because it's a waste of time and precious ink.

Maybe by now William and Emily are married, and if that's the case then I sincerely wish them the best.

My heart still aches for my mother and father at times. It aches to be home nestled in my warm comfortable bed or at the dining table listening to father discuss business practices while mother politely listens and nods while she sips her wine, her gaze lingering on the dripping candle she lights before each meal.

The ache dulls with each passing day because I have found a new purpose. To be more precise, I have found two new purposes.

Stanley Stein started a newspaper here at Carville before my arrival. Stanley is the first Jewish friend I've ever had and although he is a charismatic fellow he can be quite exhausting at times. Still, he causes me to pause and think and I like that.

The Sister in charge of job postings inquired if I would be interested in helping with the publication. She knew I was educated and capable and, furthermore, that I was bored out of my mind.

I jumped at the opportunity to write for the Star 66 and have never been sorry. Lots of women at Carville help in the infirmary or laboratory but I am not cut from that cloth. It takes a special person to care for someone in agony and I'm more inclined to tell the patient to 'buck up' which is frowned upon. It's not that I don't possess sympathy, I do. It's that I can't tolerate seeing someone else in pain and the sight of blood makes me woozy. Although I have become accustomed to the horrid forms of leprosy here, I still prefer to keep my distance if possible.

Stanley graduated from the University of Texas with a degree in pharmacology. He opened a drug store in San Antonio that was profitable, but not his dream. His dream was to be an actor or a writer. After a stint in the army he followed his dream to New York City where he worked hard and played harder as an actor in the theater district. It was there that he could no longer hide his symptoms of leprosy. He had unexplainable welts on his wrists and puffy swollen eyes that itched fiercely. When patches appeared on his face the doctor told him he had leprosy. Relieved it wasn't cancer Stanley acquiesced and came willingly to Carville.

When he arrived at what he referred to then as 'no man's land', he saw the uniformed guards and high barbed wire fences. His rights to vote, use the telephone, or mix with anyone from outside the hospital were revoked. He was determined not to live a worthless life, but to crusade on behalf of all the patients at Carville.

At first, Stanley's creation, the Star 66, was a two page printout on mimeograph paper for the patients at Carville alone. Eventually, he used the paper to campaign and change the perception of leprosy internationally. He felt the term 'leper' was derogatory and insisted it be re-labeled as "Hansen's disease" after the scientist that discovered the bacilli causing the impairment. The paper grew to include its very own dark room for developing photographs as well as a press room for conferences.

"I need your help, Faith. Can you take notes?"

"Sure, Stanley," I say, knowing full well that his eyesight is deteriorating rapidly.

"Take notes carefully because this letter is going to the president of the Veterans Association. We need their help to raise funds for new equipment, especially a press, but postage and other supplies are also necessary if we are to continue our work. I'm going to ask for their sponsorship as well. If we can reach an international audience with the VA's help, we can change the face of the disease, Faith."

"I am ready, Stanley, you may begin." I take copious notes and refrain from adding or deleting anything to Stanley's translation. His voice and way with words, hold such conviction and passion that he even convinces me the rules and regulations at Carville are preposterous. I didn't like them, but until listening to him I wasn't moved to take a stance against them.

Star 66 is not just a political rant, it also serves a social purpose for us patients. I write articles for the paper that lists weekly schedules for upcoming social activities, such as the movies and dances. We use the paper to recruit sponsors for Mardi Gras and to boast baseball team scores and upcoming tennis matches. It is also used to post the children's poetry and short stories. We even have a section called the 'Love Knot' that serves as a gossip column about possible love connections.

I find myself lying awake at night listening to the cicadas and crickets, determined to make Carville a comfortable place to reside. Building the library has become a passion project for the women in my cottage and I use a tiny segment of the paper to list any special requests for book donations. Children's books are in tall order as are the classics. Little by little the shelves are filling up and now even more patients are coming to borrow titles.

When I am not lost in a book or writing for the paper I am spending time with Jenny, my other great purpose. I have grown quite fond of her over the last few months and look forward to every minute we spend together. I found this little darling in such despair right after her brother died, she was going to run away and never come back. She longed for someone to hold her and tell her everything would be okay, and that is exactly what I did.

CHAPTER 15

SWIMMING

Jenny's smile is radiant and contagious. She is an excellent student and has taken to the piano quite well which delights her teacher, Sister Theresa. I am already planning to tell her mother about this today when we meet up with her along the fence.

"Auntie Faith," Jenny calls to me.

"Yes, dear, I'm coming," I say as I cap my pen and put it away along with my papers. I put on my walking shoes and get ready to walk with Jenny to the fence.

"What do you think she's going to bring for us today?" Jenny asks.

"I hope it's more of her homemade banana nut bread, that was divine."

"Maybe she'll have oatmeal raisin cookies!"

"One can dream…," I laugh. We often talk about food, what we miss and what we will never miss; that for Jenny is green vegetables!

"There she is. Mama!" Jenny calls to her mother who is carrying a basket of goodies as always. Luckily for Jenny her mother brings enough things for her to share, this has made her quite popular among her friends.

I give the pair time alone for a moment or two before interrupting. Jenny is lucky to have her mother's love for I believe it's what has sustained her. So many children are dumped and left at the gate, never to hear from their parents again. The stigma is too great a risk for many families.

"Faith, come look!" Jenny calls for me to come closer.

"Hello there," I say to Jane. She looks tired as always and I know life is difficult for her.

"Faith, I have brought you more banana bread, two loaves this time. I thought you could share it with the ladies in your cottage. I know some of you bake, but I had the time so I doubled the batch."

"That is very kind, Jane. Staples are hard to come by and I can assure you it won't go to waste among the ladies. How are you?"

"Carrying on," she says.

Jenny is busy looking at the treats her mother has brought so we use the time to talk woman to woman.

"How is she?"

"Her studies are coming along just fine and she is becoming quite an actress. I hope she'll agree to a role in the Christmas pageant but haven't asked yet."

"And the patches?" Jane asks.

"Five. One has broken out into pustules but it's being treated, don't worry. She hates the oil, but takes it regularly. The doctor has asked to include her in a trial. I don't have the details yet but when I do I will write everything down so you can have a look next time."

"There won't be a next time, I'm afraid," Jane whispers.

"What?"

"We've been struggling, you know that. When Jim was laid off last month things became even more difficult. He found work in Alabama and we'll be moving there in a few days. I will write, but I won't have the money to travel here."

"Jane, you have to find a way. She looks forward to your visits more than anything else."

"I know. I am hoping I can rely on you to help ease the pain. As soon as I'm able to come, you know I will. As it is now I have to sneak away from the house, Jim doesn't want me risking our reputation to be here."

"I know."

"I don't give a damn about that, let people say what they want. I have learned to develop a tough skin."

"What are you guys talking about?" Jenny interrupts.

"Darling, I won't be able to come see you for a little while. I will have to write instead."

"Mama, no!" Jenny cries and pouts, her hands clinging to the fence.

"We're moving to Alabama, your daddy found a job there and we have to do what's best for the family. Times are very tough."

"It's not fair," Jenny says.

"Life isn't fair," I interject for perspective.

"I'll be sure to send you a Christmas package and pray I am able to visit in the new year."

"Mama?"

"It'll be okay, Jenny. We'll have lots to do to keep busy until then. Why before you know it, it will be Thanksgiving and then Christmas, we'll have a pageant and you'll be required to attend lots of rehearsals if you want a starring role," I say.

"Yes! I want a starring role!"

"Wonderful, and before you know it, I'll see you both again."

Jane and Jenny hug as best as they can through the fence. A guard passes by but is kind enough to leave us alone.

We say our goodbyes and walk back to my cottage to unpack the goodies. I slice the banana bread and put it on a plate for everyone to enjoy. There are peaches and spiced pecans, berry jam, cookies, and even chocolates. Jenny gives me a piece of chocolate and a few peaches and takes the rest to share with her friends.

In the evening, after supper and church, we walk back to the fence and slip underneath using the hole. It may be our last chance to swim because it's nearly October and there is a nip in the air, making the water chilly.

"Brrr," I say when I dip my big toe in the water's edge.

"I am just going to jump right in," Jenny declares. She takes off her clothing and gets a running start before leaping right into the water, making a huge splash.

I wade in more slowly, allowing the water to inch up my body ever so slowly, like a seductress.

"You there!" A man calls out.

"Jenny, duck down."

The two of us are forced to go under water. Jenny can hold her breath longer than I can, so when I come to the surface for air I am the first to notice the uniformed guard.

"Get out. You are not allowed across the fence," he says rather sternly.

"Can you just let us have a quick swim, no one will know but you?" I plead.

"I'll lose my job. Oh, alright, I reckon I can give you a few minutes…," he says giving in.

Jenny and I float on our backs and stare at the gibbous moon, it's a pretty night made brighter by the stars.

"Come on now, let's go."

The guard has lost his patience with us so we swim back to shore towards the rock where we left our clothes. The guard turns around to give us privacy and when we are dressed he escorts us back across the fence.

"I will be mending that hole in the morning so don't get any more ideas, ya hear?" he warns.

"Yes, Sir."

The guards eyes linger on mine a second too long. He looks about my age and is handsome in a rugged sort of way. He wears a short beard and has curly hair that falls to his shirt collar. His eyes are a startling blue. I am overwhelmed by a feeling I can't describe. It's as if this man has a role to play in my life, but that can't be possible because I don't even know his name.

CHAPTER 16

BRADLEY

"I thought I told you not to swim?" the guard says a few days later when he approaches me in the water at night.

"You did. Are you going to turn me in?"

"Are you trying to get me in trouble? This is my watch and I could lose my job."

"Alright, turn around and I'll get out," I say reluctantly.

He turns his back to me and I step lightly from the water, rubbing the mud off my feet when I reach the grass. I didn't bring a towel so I slip my cotton shirt over my shoulders and step into my skirt before sitting on the rock to put on my shoes.

"Are you decent?"

"Yes, you can turn around, you sure know how to ruin a good time."

"You call swimming in the freezing river a good time?"

"Yes, I do. There isn't much else to do around here these days." I have finished all my articles for the paper and Jenny is busy with rehearsals so I've had more time on my hands than I know what to do with.

"It's probably my civic duty to show you what a real good time is," he says teasing me.

"That would be lovely, what do you have in mind?" I say, playing along.

"Well, if you don't mind waiting here, I get off in an hour and I'll take you to "Red's".

"What's that? A bar?"

"More or less, I've seen several patients there, must be they are all crawling under the same damn spot," he laughs.

"You don't turn them in?"

"Nah, they aren't hurting anyone and they always come back."

"Good point. Sure, I'll meet you back here in an hour. I'd like to go change if you don't mind," I say, needing to get out of my wet shirt that's clinging to my skin.

"It's a date. I'm Bradley by the way. Bradley Jackson," he says shaking my cold shriveled hand.

"See you in an hour," I say wondering what the heck just happened while I walked home.

"Ladies, you won't believe this but I just got asked on a date by a guard!"

Marilyn and Anne, Mary and Louise, all surround me to hear how things unfolded between Bradley and me. The ladies are divided about what I should do. Beverly is already in her closet picking out a scarf that she insists I wear, while Mary warns me not to go.

"He could be after your virtue, Faith, and that's all you have left," she reminds me knowing full well I am a virgin.

"He can have it. Gosh, to feel a man's arms around me again, I never thought it could happen!" I laugh and my friends laugh with me.

"I have some blusher in my room, and red lipstick too!" Anne says, and the ladies all stand around and watch me get ready for my date. I wear my svelte, body hugging knee length black skirt with a matching shirt that has flouncy butterfly sleeves. Beverly's scarf is tied carefully around my neck and I apply the blusher and lipstick. I sweep my hair up into a loose bun and when I steal a glimpse of myself in the mirror I think I look downright radiant.

"If I don't come back before midnight it means I'm having a good time. Aww, Mary, don't worry, I am sure we'll just be dancing and chatting. I promise I won't let him steal my virtue," I say to my friend.

I meet Bradley at the fence and he parts the gate for me so I don't ruin my outfit. We walk along the river talking about the weather and other silly things until we get to his car that's parked a half mile down the path. He opens the passenger side door for me to get in and we're off.

"Are you nervous?" he asks, his hands gripping the steering wheel.

"Not at all, are you?"

"Yes. I'll be nervous for both of us."

Bradley drives me to a ramshackle building with a sign out front in bold letters reading, Reds. Inside we are seated in a wooden booth and served beer on tap. I never liked beer, but tonight I have every intention of drinking it. It's not every night I manage an escape with an escort.

"So, Bradley, tell me about yourself."

"I grew up in Fullerton, Louisiana, have you ever heard of it?"

"No, I haven't. Go on."

"It's a ghost town now, used to be a lumber town back in the day but most people have abandoned it and dispersed. My folks were lucky to find jobs at Carville and as soon as I finished school I got a job too. That was about six months ago…"

"So that's why I haven't seen you around, you're new."

"I'm still learning the ropes. I suppose I'll have to play dumb if we run into anyone tonight," he jokes.

"Why did you want to bring me here anyway, do you have a soft spot for escapees?"

"Just for you," he says looking down at his beer and then taking a big gulp. He has a frothy mustache from the suds and mops it with a napkin.

"That's kind. Thank you for letting Jenny and me finish our swim a few nights ago."

"Is she your sister?"

"She is a special friend, she's all alone here. I found her one night by the river planning her escape. She wanted to run away all by her little self."

"You stopped her, why?"

"The swim may have killed her, and she's far too young to manage on her own."

"Agreed, poor thing." Bradley was empathetic to Jenny's plight, "Where is her family? Do they visit?" he asks.

"Her mother did for a while, but she can't anymore because they moved away. Luckily Jenny will be busy for a while with the pageant and all." I explain the upcoming holiday extravaganza and pageant to Bradley.

"It sounds like quite an event, at least there are things to do inside, I can't imagine being cooped up."

"We also have Mardi Gras, the guards sponsor a child every year and we make a big float which requires a good deal of planning, that's fun too," I say.

"What else? Tell me more."

"It's changed quite a bit in the year I've been here, there is a more jovial atmosphere nowadays if you can imagine. We have all sorts of clubs, and there is the choir and resident band. We have tennis, baseball, bicycles, and of course the children go to school. There's the paper, that's what I do…"

"Are you a writer?" He interrupts me with his question.

"I am not sure I'd call myself a writer, but I do put together articles for the paper, I am sort of the editor-at-large. Usually I post upcoming activities, schedules, obituaries, things like that. I also help Stanley when he is working on a project; we just finished his big push to the VA for funding. He's something else…"

"I've heard about him, he's quite the crusader and lobbyist."

"He really is. I admire his spunk, he refuses to let anything get him down, which is refreshing."

"I imagine it's challenging day in and day out, I mean I just work the perimeter so I don't see a lot of patients, but when I do my heart sinks."

"Is it sinking right now?" I tease.

"You're different, I mean you don't look like you have it, ya know?"

"Well, I do. I am not disfigured like some of the patients, but I have numb patches and some issues with sensitivity," I admit, and suddenly I feel self conscious.

"Well, I give you a lot of credit, a pretty young girl such as yourself…" his voice trails off and he sips more beer.

"You don't have to feel sorry for me, I've accepted my fate. I am a patient and that's not going to change anytime soon, all I can do is make the best of my situation. Some days it's harder than others. I admit, this feels nice though, being outside the fence."

"Cheers," Bradley says and we clink our mugs before ordering another round.

The beer is making me giddy and eager to dance. Bradley is light on his feet and makes an excellent partner. I admit I am happy when a slow song comes on and he draws me close to his chest. He smells like a mixture of cigars and cedar. It's very manly and I have an urge to kiss him.

"Would you permit me to kiss you?" he asks as if reading my mind.

"On our first date and in front of all the patrons?" I tease.

"I have a better idea, let's get some air." He takes my hand and walks me outside into the fresh, chilly night air. He drapes his coat across my shoulders and pulls me to him. He doesn't hesitate to kiss me full on the mouth. His lips are soft and seeking, his caress on my shoulders light and confident. When we pull apart, his eyes search mine and I nod in permission. He kisses me deeper this time, introducing his tongue with light flicks. His muscular arms protect me against the chill and keep me up while I'm feeling light headed.

"I suppose I should get you back, huh?" he asks.

"Probably," I agree.

"I wouldn't want to take advantage of you, in fact I apologize, Faith."

"For what? For kissing me and making me feel human?"

"Some would think it was improper is all."

"Well I don't care what people think, kiss me again, please." Feeling his desire press up against me makes me feel like a woman and it's the best gift I've received in over a year.

Bradley holds my hand and kisses my palm before opening the passenger side car door for me. We drive in silence back to the hospital and he walks me to the fence although I tell him he doesn't need to.

"I insist," he says treating me like a lady.

I arrive home shortly after midnight and find several of the women waiting up for me in their pajamas.

"Well? How did it go?" They ask and motion for me to sit in the middle of them.

"Better than I could have ever imagined."

"You're glowing, Faith."

"We danced and talked, and kissed …"

"Oh my!" The ladies giggle and listen to every detail of my night out on the town. After an hour of discussion we finally turn in. I had forgotten how it feels to be happy, and now that I remember , I want more of it.

***

My days are spent between helping Jenny practice her lines for the pageant and helping with set design. It's going to be very elaborate and the artist in residence has recruited me to help her with props. I count the hours until eight o'clock when I slip away from the cottage and meet Bradley by the fence. Sometimes we spend our time together driving around town listening to the radio, other times we park and talk. Once in a while we go dancing, but I am increasingly afraid one of us will be noticed and get in trouble.

"I want to show you off," Bradley says to me tonight, "you are so beautiful."

"Thank you, Bradley. You aren't so bad yourself," I tease.

"May I take you dancing? We can go to Reds again, it's not too far."

"I just don't want anyone to recognize me, or you for that matter."

"I can go in first and scope the place, how about that? If it's clear we can sit in the corner booth and have a drink and do some dancing."

"Okay, let's do it."

Bradley goes in before me and waves me towards him after he has checked the place out.

"It's a ghost town in there, maybe four or five folks at the bar, but that's it," he says.

He puts his arm around my shoulder and the waitress shows us to our table in the corner. She brings a round of beers and says she'll be back to take our order. I don't want anything from the menu, I only want to stare into the face of the man across from me. I sip my drink and tap my feet in time with the music.

"Do you ever think about getting out of here? You know, escaping?" he asks.

"No, not really, mostly because I don't want to hurt my family."

"What have they done for you? For all you know, they may not even live here anymore."

"You could be right. I can't leave though, I need my medicine and I'm enrolled in an upcoming study. People depend upon me," I say.

"I just wish I could get you out of there. We could move somewhere together so we don't have to sneak around. I really like you, Faith. I'd like you to be my girl," he says, reaching across the table and taking my hands in his own.

The door opens and several of the uniformed guards from the hospital enter the bar.

"Shit," I say sliding down my seat, hoping none of them will recognize me in this environment.

"Hey there, Bradley, who's the lucky lady?" One of the guards who works a shift with Bradley makes his way over to us and squeezes in beside Bradley in the booth.

"Hi, Harold, this is Amanda," he lies, and I realize it's going to be hard to keep my names straight.

"She's a looker alright, care to dance?" he asks me.

"Harold, she's with me, if she dances with anyone, it'll be me," Bradley says puffing his chest.

"Some guys have all the luck; I had to ask. Y'all have a good evening now," he says proceeding to the bar to drink with the other guards.

"Phew, that was a close call, maybe we should just go?"

"I don't think they recognize you, we're okay. If we rush out of here it will just arouse suspicion. Let's enjoy our drinks and then we'll leave."

When we stand to leave, Harold approaches us again, "I recognize you from somewhere, did you go to the university?" he asks.

"No, you must have me confused," I respond.

"I'll figure it out," he says wagging his finger in front of me.

We say goodnight to Harold and leave the bar, my nerves are

frazzled and even Bradley who is ordinarily calm and collected is shaken.

"That was close, I'm sorry for bringing you here and putting you in a bad situation."

"It's a risk every time we leave, but it's worth it," I smile and lean into Bradley.

"So, will you be my girl?" he asks.

"What does the job entail?" I joke. "Of course, I'd love to be your girl." Bradley is like a fever I feel all over, warming me from head to toe.

CHAPTER 17

MEDICAL TRIALS

I wish my medical trials weren't in the middle of the holiday preparations. When I signed up to volunteer I hadn't met Bradley and therefore had nothing to lose. If there is a silver lining it's that I am only enrolled in the bath trials and they aren't supposed to be too taxing. Other patients are experiencing lots of adverse side effects as a result of trying new medications and they look and feel dreadful.

Every day I have to submerge my naked body into a hot bath, exposing only my head. Normally I find water to be a tonic, but in this circumstance it's not. The water is scalding hot and threatens to burn my skin. I advance from the baths to the "hot box" in the second phase of my trial. The boxes are made for us patients to stand up in while naked. My entire body, except for my head, is in the box and the temperature is steadily increased over the course of three hours. The idea is to raise a patient's body temperature to dangerous heights to see how it affects the disease.

I am monitored before and after each daily session, by the end of the week I feel so unhealthy that I want to die. I am dehydrated and exhausted and barely able to care for myself. The heat saps my body of vital nutrients, I am sure of it for my urine is a rusty color. I'm instructed to drink a gallon of water each day, but on Friday all I can do is sleep. I'm physically unable to meet Bradley and pray he understands.

I watch a cockroach scamper across the floorboards in my room and make no move to retrieve it. I close my eyes, shut out the world, and sleep for sixteen hours straight. I am awakened by someone knocking at the door; sweet little Jenny has been worried about me and the ladies can't keep her out of my room any longer.

"Auntie, are you okay?" she asks.

"Oh, honey, I'll be alright. I had some hard tests this week is all," I explain.

"Are you going to die?"

"Heaven's no, why would you think that?"

"Dorothy said you might die, she said sometimes people die when they volunteer for the experiments."

"I don't know if that's true or not, but I'm still here, come give me a hug," she puts the mug of tea she prepared on the bedside table and clings to me.

"Crawl in," I say lifting the covers. We snuggle for a little bit and both of us fall back to sleep for the better part of an hour.

The dinner bell rings in the distance and I realize I'm starving.

"Let's go together, I just need to visit the bathroom quickly. I splash my face with cold water and though I am woozy and pale, I am determined not to frighten Jenny.

When I get back to the room I drink the tea that Jenny flavored with lemon and honey and then we walk towards the dining hall. Jenny is learning to ride a bicycle, but today we walk since I am not up to the task of running beside her. My muscles are fatigued and I feel faint. I feel the need to rest and sit on the bench that's midway between my cottage and the dining hall to catch my breath. Sister Audry sees me and hurries over to assist.

"Hold on to my shoulders and we'll take you to the infirmary, Dr. Jo will want to see you," she says.

"Don't worry, honey, I'll be okay. Look for Dorothy or one of the ladies from the cottage, okay?"

"Don't die, Faith!" she cries into her hands. Luckily, Mary is close by and is more than willing to enjoy dinner with Jenny while I see the doctor.

The doctor sees me at once, and after a thorough examination he prescribes vitamins to restore my system, rest, and lots of water. He also wants me to remain indoors until I feel restored. The air is nippy nowadays and he doesn't want me to get sick and develop pneumonia.

"Your trial days are over for now. Apparently the heat doesn't agree with your system," Dr. Jo says while he pricks my fingers. My fingers don't even feel the needle he pokes to get blood, and I swear my index finger and pinkie on my right hand are shorter now.

"It's from nerve damage, Faith. The disease invades the nervous system and causes a loss of sensation. When this occurs the digits reabsorb into the hand, it's peculiar and we don't understand it yet. I suggest you drink tea and hot coffee using your left hand from now on. Because you lack sensitivity on the right, you won't feel temperatures and can burn yourself badly enough to cause a much more serious problem requiring amputation."

"Okay, Doctor, I promise to get my rest. How is Jenny? I mean Diana? I'm sorry, I call her Jenny although I know everyone else refers to her as Diana."

"She is doing well, we're watching the skin on her legs and arms carefully. We are treating them with an ointment made from the chaulmoogra oil mixed with lard. So far it's keeping it from spreading."

"That's what they used for my abscess and it worked well. Thank you for taking care of her, she's like a sister to me," I say.

"Yes, I know. She talks about you all the time when she's here for her appointments. It sounds like the play is coming along, I can't wait to attend."

"Will your wife be with you again this year?" I ask.

"She wouldn't miss it."

Sister Audry has a wheelchair ready for me when my appointment is over. "It's just until you get stronger, maybe a few days, okay?" she asks.

"It's okay, I need it. I thought I was going to faint earlier," I admit.

"I'll bring you home now and have Mary bring you back some dinner. All I want you to do is rest, understand?"

"Yes, I do. I won't even attend mass this evening, and although I have no appetite I know it's important to eat a little something."

"God will understand."

Once I am tucked back in bed I fall right to sleep. I dream of a house along a peaceful riverbed. I am swimming but something keeps pulling me under. I wake up coughing and drowning in mucous and fluid. I have developed a fever overnight as well. I am too weak to call any of my housemates so I close my eyes and pray.

"God, please don't let me die. Jenny needs me, and I need to be here for her." The little girl is my first and most pressing thought.

In the morning Mary checks on me, "You were coughing all night," she complains.

"I don't feel so well," I say, listening to the rattling in my chest.

She presses a palm to my forehead and tells me I am burning up. She helps me dress and wheels me to the infirmary where Dr. Jo is waiting.

"You have fluid in your lungs, which means you most likely have pneumonia. I won't know for certain until I examine your sputum. Is it hard to get a deep breath?"

"It is, it feels like there is a shelf in my chest and I can't get past it." As I breathe in and out we both hear the whistle coming from my lungs and the doctor tells me I am wheezing.

"You'll need to sit up in bed and spit out any phlegm you cough up. I'll have the nurse give you a bucket before you leave. Drink plenty of water and get your rest. If you are willing, I'd like to try a new method of treatment that they are using to treat pneumonia in Boston with great results."

"What is the procedure?" I ask.

"I would inject you with emulsified olive oil directly into your veins. The oil should absorb the pneumonia and any other toxins in your bloodstream. The poisons will adhere to the globules and then lose their potency. Your temperature should drop within twenty-four to forty-eight hours. You should be entirely well in three to four weeks. Faith, I don't want to frighten you, but pneumonia is serious, don't hesitate to see me if you aren't getting better. I'll have one of the Sisters check on you every morning and night."

"Okay, you can try it. If it helps me, hopefully it will help someone else too."

"That's the spirit, let me have a moment to prepare the syringe and I'll be back." The doctor leaves the room and I am so exhausted I can barely keep my eyes open. The procedure is only minimally invasive and not any more painful then having blood drawn. Luckily I have good veins.

My chest rattles and feels heavy, but I do as Dr. Jo instructs and prop myself up in bed to help ease the pain. Mary pokes her head in my room just as I am nodding off, "You have a visitor," she says.

Bradley walks in my small room and closes the door behind him. I should feel embarrassed to have him here but I don't. I don't care what state my room is in, or how my hair looks, I only want to be held.

"Darling, you look awful," he says truthfully.

"I feel worse," I say and then release a cough so deep it pierces my chest and burns afterward.

"What do you need? Some more pillows? Here, I have an idea …" he crawls in bed behind me and leans his back against the wall, now I have him and the pillows to prop me up. He rubs his hands through my oily hair and hums a song I don't recognize. It feels wonderful to be cared for, to be touched.

"What have they done to you?" he asks.

"It was the hot box that did me in, now we know that doesn't work, at least for me."

"Let me take you away from here, please. I can take care of you…"

I think I hear Bradley say, I love you, but perhaps it is only in my dreams.

CHAPTER 18

LOVE

They say that love is the best antidote and now I understand why. Bradley refuses to leave my side while I am sick and takes care of me with the gentleness of a mother. He insists on being the one at my bedside even if it means breaking the rules and losing his job.

Men aren't allowed in the women's quarters as a rule. However, many of the women in my cottage have boyfriends and we always manage to sneak them in and keep the affair secret, Bradley is no exception.

I suppose it's fate that Bradley is caught coming and going from my residence. When he is detained and questioned by Dr. Jo he tells the truth. He confesses his love for me to Dr. Jo and explains his desire to take care of me and be sure I have everything I need, especially at night. Dr. Jo is not only concerned about propriety, but he worries about Bradley being in close proximity to me, risking his own health. Bradley lost his job as a result of the offense, but Dr. Jo turns a blind eye to the fact he sneaks in which allows him more time to dote on me and help me restore my health.

When my lungs are stronger and I no longer cough up phlegm or wheeze, we take short walks to strengthen my legs that have become soft and feel like Jello. Bradley holds my hand and leads me towards the lake where we sit and chat for long expanses of time, talking about our future, strengthening our bond. I find him to be incredibly smart and interesting, not to mention sweet and caring.

"Maybe we can get married? Then they would have to let me live inside Carville with you. We could build a small cottage on

Main Street on Cottage Row if we have to," he says.

"I don't think they'll allow it, Bradley. Besides, what kind of a life would that be for you in here with all of us?" I ask, not wanting my feelings for Bradley to cloud my judgment.

"Don't you understand by now that I love you, Faith? I want to spend my life with you. It would be my honor to have you as my wife. I know we've only known each other for a few months but I've never felt this way about anyone before."

"Is that a proposal?" I ask. Our relationship has progressed very quickly, but it feels comfortable and natural.

"Well, I don't have a ring yet and I don't know whose blessing to seek. Should I call your father first?"

"I don't need a fancy ring, all I need is your commitment. You've certainly showed me that you will take care of me in sickness and health, for better or worse. As for my father, he hasn't reached out to me once. I feel the same way, Bradley, I'm head over heels for you, but what will your family say?" I can't help the ache that explodes in my chest when I think of my family. They have abandoned me completely and it has left a hole in my heart with deep seated psychological implications. A hole that Bradley fills. Still, there is his family to consider.

"Come here, Faith, let me hold you. We will be each other's family now; it will be you and me against the world. Your family is more concerned with themselves and the stigma of the disease than they are with your welfare. That's not love, my dear, that's selfishness and conceit. As for my family, I know we haven't discussed them much and there is a reason for that. I'm afraid my mother died from breast cancer several years ago and my father not long after. He had a horrible farming accident that took him instantly. I've been on my own for a while, but if there is one thing I know it's that they would have loved you and they would approve of our marriage. I do have another thought I want to discuss though."

"I'm so sorry, Bradley. Why didn't you tell me before?"

"I don't talk about the past very often, but I want you to know who I am and where I come from. My folks were hard working people, we weren't rich by any means but we had what we needed to get by. My father always told me not to let any man outwork me, he had a work ethic like no one else I've ever known. That's how he was able to support us and it defined him. He was a truly good man and my parents were in love. They never had other children, it was just the three of us. After my mom died a few years ago, my dad threw himself even harder into his work. Sometimes he even missed eating dinner and supper with me, but I knew it was painful for him to be at the table and see my mom's empty chair. There was speculation that he caused the accident that took his life. I will never know for sure if that's true, but I know it was excruciating for him to live without her day in and day out. His heart was broken."

I hug Bradley and inhale his musky scent. "You said you had something else to discuss?"

"I think we should include Jenny in our family, she needs us."

"Oh, Bradley. That would be wonderful. I just don't want to get ahead of ourselves, I'm certain they won't let you live here, marriage isn't sanctioned at Carville, you know that."

"Perhaps we should think about getting you out of here then?"

"But Jenny takes several medications, not just the chaulmoogra oil and capsules. She is injected with proteins and has glandular extracts monthly. Dependent upon how she responds, Dr. Jo has discussed milk injections and even a transfusion of blood plasma for her. My program will be easy enough to sustain, right now my diet is merely fat free and high in protein. "

"You could stockpile your medications until Christmas and we'll plan to get you out of here in the new year."

"I don't know, it's rather risky. How will I get my hands on Jenny's medicine? I don't feel right stealing anything."

"I don't know, but staying here has its risks too. The "hot box" nearly took your life. I don't want you in any more trials and Jenny shouldn't be either. We can stay at my apartment for the time being and when I save enough money we'll move. We can go anywhere you want, the world is our oyster."

"New Orleans?" I ask.

"Sure, why not? No one would guess you have leprosy, Faith. You have no deformities and neither does Jenny. We can make it work."

"You really love me that much?" I ask.

"I really do. Will you marry me, Faith?" Bradley kneels down on one knee and takes my hands in his. His eyes search mine for an answer.

"I will."

We kiss and hold one another for a long time. I don't know how Jenny will react or if she will be willing to leave with us, and I am not entirely certain I want to leave. At least in here there are doctors studying the disease. Outside the fence people are cruel, if anyone ever found us out we'd be in deep trouble.

CHAPTER 19

WEDDING PLANS

Thanksgiving is finally here. The staff has outdone themselves with a fine meal that has everyone salivating. The tables are set with fancy lace tablecloths, candles, silverware, and napkins; some even have decorative cornucopias at the center. There are a dozen turkeys with gravy and plenty of side dishes that include rice, corn, and beans. Best of all is the gramophone playing throughout the meal.

"That was outstanding but now I'm ridiculously full!" I say to Jenny after we've good and stuffed ourselves. Mass is at one o'clock today and we have a few minutes beforehand to chat.

"Me too," she says placing a hand across her bulging belly. "Sister Anne says there will be even more food tonight, more turkey, and cakes, and pies too!"

"Hopefully they will keep the gramophone playing so we can do some dancing," I say as I twirl Jenny around under my arms.

"I think the doctors are dressing up like pilgrims and performing a skit."

"You don't say? How fun. I'd like to see that!"

"Then it will be almost Christmastime!"

"My favorite time of the year, next to my birthday of course," I say.

"Do you think Santa will come to Carville?"

"I have no doubt that he will! He would never leave any of the children out. Jenny, sit for a minute." I motion for Jenny to sit beside me on a bench deciding this might be a good time to discuss my upcoming marriage with her.

"I have something to talk to you about. You know how special you are to me, right?"

"I do."

"I think of you as my very own niece or little sister. We've known each other for over a year now and I think you feel the same way about me. I can't replace your mother and would never want to because she loves you dearly. It's hard for our families, even if they love us and want us to be with them, we simply can't be because it could put them at risk. Having said that, I want you as part of my family and so does Bradley."

"But Bradley doesn't have leprosy," she says confused.

"He doesn't, you're right. However, he loves me and has asked me to marry him. He cares about you too and wants the three of us to be a family. It will have to be a secret though because Carville doesn't sanction marriage."

"You'll make a pretty bride, Faith!"

"I don't know about all of that, but we are getting married tomorrow evening. I am sneaking through the fence and we are going to the justice of the peace to say our vows. Bradley wants to take us away from Carville, he wants us to move far away from all of this," I motion with my arms to our hopeless surroundings. Granted today is special, but most days are challenging.

"When you say, 'us', you mean me too?"

"You don't have to come. The decision is yours, but I think you and I are healthy enough to leave this place. You can go to a regular school and make new friends. We'll have a house and Bradley will provide for us, I know it."

"But what about my family? What happens if my mama tries to find me and I'm not here?"

"I've thought about that too. We can leave word with Mary telling her how to get in touch with us. We'll get a P.O. box right away so she can write us at once if your mother sends you mail or comes looking for you."

"What about Dorothy? She's my best friend, she has trouble

getting around now because of her feet."

"I know you care about Dorothy and so do I. She will always be your special friend. We can ask the Sisters to have a special pair of Carville clogs made for her twisted feet, I'll pay for them myself. I have saved all of my Carville coins and have no other use for them."

"She'd like that because right now she can only wear socks and she hates it."

"I'll give you some time to think about all of this, I know it's overwhelming. We aren't leaving right away, but we'd like to be in our new home by Christmas."

"Will we have a tree and stockings?" she asks.

"Of course we will," I promise.

"I don't need to think about it, I want to come. Even though we'll miss Mardi Gras," she quips and I think she and I are kindred rebels.

"Remember it has to be kept a secret, okay? You can't even tell Dorothy," I say ignoring the comment about Mardi Gras.

"I cross my heart and hope to die, stick a needle in my eye."

"Very well, then. Let's get inside for mass."

.

CHAPTER 20

MARRIAGE

Mary and Lynette, my closest friends, are the only ones aside from Jenny that know I'm sneaking out and getting married tonight. I admit that while I am over the moon, I am also nervous.

Mary lends me her favorite pearl stud earrings so that I have something 'old' and 'borrowed', Lynette gives me a blue scrap of material cut into the shape of a heart, now I just need something new. New is hard to come by in Carville, but my friends remind me my ring will be new.

They help me select an outfit for my wedding that is suitable and tell me what to expect at night. I don't plan to sneak back into Carville until the early morning hours when the guards are changing shifts. Bradley is preparing his apartment to accommodate us this evening so that we can spend our first night as man and wife together.

Lynette is married with two children at home so I ask her about my duties in bed.

"Will it hurt?" I ask about lovemaking.

"Not if he is gentle, and I am sure he will be."

"What do I do? I've never done more than kiss?"

"It will all come naturally, just don't be afraid," she says.

"And don't lay there like a log either, men don't like that," Mary interjects.

"How would you know?" I ask, knowing full well she has never been married.

"Just because I'm not married doesn't mean I am a prude for heaven's sake."

The three of us eat dinner together at eleven a.m. and then

I go home for a shower. I shave my legs so that they are nice and smooth. I spend extra time styling my hair and when I'm satisfied I use Lynette's blusher on my cheeks. I tuck the lipstick and the blue heart into my clutch so I have them for the ceremony and say my goodbyes. The ladies are going to tell Sister Audry that I am resting comfortably in bed tonight rather than attending mass.

At one o'clock I use my ability to vanish and slip behind the cottage unnoticed. I walk quietly towards the river, looking over my shoulder to make sure no one is following me. A couple of men are walking on the levee so I duck behind a tree until they've passed. When no one is around I crawl beneath the gate and run towards the road. Bradley's already there waiting for me.

"You look beautiful, Faith. Shall we?" he asks holding his arm out to me, eager to start the ceremony.

"We shall." I notice how dapper Bradley looks today in a suit coat and tie. He shaved his beard and mustache and trimmed his hair as well.

Walking into the town hall, I feel butterflies in my stomach.

"Are you okay?" Bradley asks.

"I am better than okay," I assure him even though what we are about to do is risky.

The gentleman presiding over our ceremony is slight in stature and has a pimple on his nostril that I can't keep my eyes from. His secretary acts as our witness for the proceedings and I have the sense she has done this before.

We face each other and repeat our vows.

"I, Faith Cooper, take you, Bradley Jackson, to be my husband, to have and to hold from this day forward, for better or for worse, for richer, for poorer, in sickness and in health to love and to cherish; from this day forward until death do us part," I say with tear-filled eyes.

"I, Bradley Jackson, take you, Faith Cooper, to be my wife, to have and to hold from this day forward, for better or for worse, for richer, for poorer, in sickness and in health to love and to cherish; from this day forward until death do us part," he says reaching into his pocket for the rings.

He slides a sterling silver band over my knuckle onto my ring finger. It is a simple ring with nothing but today's date engraved on the inside. When it's my turn to place his ring, my hands tremble and I nearly drop it, but manage to maintain my composure and slide it on his finger.

"You may kiss your bride," the justice of the peace says.

Bradley places his hands on my shoulders and pulls me closer to him, he leans down and tilts my chin upwards to be in line with his. He brushes his lips across mine, gently, then presses his lips to mine. He tastes like peppermint and hope.

We hold hands as we leave the town office building and walk to his apartment, which is not more than three-quarters of a mile away. Bradley stops me in front of a red brick house with gables and wrought iron fixtures. We climb a set of stairs off the back of the home and Bradley gets out his keys to unlock the door. He lifts me into his arms and carries me across the threshold into his humble apartment.

"It's for good luck," he explains when he puts me down.

His space is small and lacks decorations, but it's tidy and comfortable. The kitchen table has been set with china, flowers, and candles. I can smell a roast beef cooking and know that Bradley put a great deal of effort into making this a special day.

"Are you hungry? We can eat now if you want."

"I'm hungry, but I'd rather you kiss me," I admit, although it's forward of me.

"How about a glass of champagne and a toast first?"

"Yes, please," I am grateful he had the foresight to buy champagne.

"To my wife, Mrs. Faith Jackson, may we always seek the silver linings," he says.

"Cheers, to silver linings," I say clinking my glass to his, appreciative of his simple words.

The champagne slides down my throat and helps to put me at ease. Bradley takes my glass and places it beside his on the counter. He kisses me deeply and carries me to his room. Rose petals cover the bedspread and candles line the dresser.

"I'll light these first," he says.

"Okay," I answer nervously.

Bradley strikes a match and lights the wicks. I am not sure what to do; do I undress myself or does he do that?

We sit on the edge of the bed in awkward silence. Bradley lifts my feet and takes off my shoes one at a time. He rolls down my stockings and pulls me to a standing position. We kiss a little and I feel his need pressing against my stomach.

"I don't want to do anything that makes you uncomfortable."

"We're married now, Bradley. We're meant to be together, it's just I've never seen a naked man before."

"And I've never seen a naked woman, not one that belongs to me anyways," he grins.

He unbuttons the collar of my blouse and pushes it off my shoulders. He kisses my neck and collarbones and nibbles on my ear. It feels heavenly and I nearly swoon I am so caught up in the sensation.

"Steady now," he warns.

"I'm afraid my knees buckled when you were doing that…"

"What? This?" Bradley nibbles at my neck and unbuttons my blouse all the way, exposing my bra and belly. He pushes it off my shoulders and traps me, arms behind my back, while he speckles me with kisses up and down my chest, belly, and neck. I lean into him, wanting more but feeling suddenly shy and inexperienced. I don't want to appear clumsy.

"Darling, just relax and love me," he says.

I follow my husband's lead and return his kisses. I remove his belt and untuck his shirt. My hands are chilly but I slide them under his shirt, up his back, and lean against his chest to close the gap between us. He lifts me on the bed and finishes undressing me, one garment at a time. When I am naked he stands back and asks permission to look.

"You're beautiful, your skin, it's so soft and perfect." He cups my small breasts in his hands and rubs his thumb across my nipples sending a sensation rippling through me that fills me with desire. I undress my husband and admire his sinewy body. He is lean and muscular, strong, and mine.

I've never been touched by a man this way, but Bradley is tender and loving. He prepares me for what is to come and I invite him to make love to me by opening my legs. I can't tell if Bradley enjoys me or not, his head is buried in my shoulders and he's grunting like he's in pain.

"Are you alright, how does it feel?" he asks me.

"I am okay, it feels fine," I answer honestly. It stings a little bit, but I am trying to focus on the burning sensation coming deeper from within. It's like an itch that needs to be scratched.

Bradley thrusts deeper into me, he holds my hands above my head and in minutes it's over. He pulls out and lays on his backside. I want and need more, the itch hasn't been scratched, instead it's spreading.

Bradley senses this and rolls to his side, he begins to caress my mound, slowly inserting his fingers into my womanhood, rubbing them along my pubic bone until I am breathing heavy. In seconds I climax, blood rushes through my body and my legs shake uncontrollably.

"Is that the first time you've climaxed?" he asks.

"Yes, it's the first anyone's ever touched me, you know that."

"Well, we men sort of take care of ourselves when we need to…"

"Hmm, it never occurred to me, and now I have you anyway," I say positioning myself on my side to face him.

"I do believe I love you, Mrs. Jackson."

"And I love you, thank you for making me your wife," I say and we start the lovers dance all over.

JENNY

CHAPTER 21

SECRETS

I have a secret and I can't even tell my best friend, Dorothy. Even though it's not Christmas yet I go to the Canteen and use my Carville coins to buy her as much candy as I can. I put all the goodies in a basket that Faith gave me and tie it up with a bright red ribbon.

"Hi Dorothy!" I say with mixed emotions, this is the last time I will see my friend because we are leaving tonight.

"Hi there," Dorothy says looking like she is down in the dumps.

"I brought you a present. " I hand her the basket that overflows with more sweets than you can imagine.

"Golly, what's all this for?"

"You're my best friend and I know you are sad. I just want to cheer you up!" I exclaim.

Dorothy is wheelchair-bound now, her feet are so twisted that she can't walk anymore. She hates relying on people to take her anywhere but I never mind, so I get behind the chair and push her outside. We walk over to the tennis courts and watch a few women hit the ball for awhile. When we're bored, we watch the baseball team practice.

"You're hands are in good shape, Dorothy, you can take piano lessons if you want," I suggest.

"Maybe."

"Or you could knit? You could make shawls for everyone and sell them too, then you'll be rich!"

"I don't know, I think I'll help design the Mardi Gras float this year. I'll be good at that."

"That will be so fun, you have to get a sponsor, who can you ask? Maybe your favorite nurse?"

"Yep, I know Mrs. Reese will support me, and then you can help me come up with ideas," she says.

"Yes, oh no, look at the time! I have to go now, I'm meeting Faith." I wheel Dorothy back to her room as fast as I can. My departure is quick, but I am so afraid I am gonna spill the beans that I have to leave right away.

***

When everyone at Carville has turned in for the night, I sneak across the hospital grounds to meet Faith at her cottage. Mary, Anne, Beverly, and Lynette are all waiting up to say goodbye to me. Mary promises to be on the look out for any mail from my mother and to get word to me right away if there is any news. The ladies hug us goodbye and we are off.

It's pitch black out tonight, and a thick fog has rolled in. We can hear the foghorn on the river and follow our well worn path to the fence. We duck under the fence and walk a little ways until we get to the spot where the river bends. Bradley is already waiting for us there.

"Hi, squirt."

"Hi, Uncle Bradley," I answer back.

"Hop in," he says holding the door open for me.

Faith and I both get in the front seat and I'm so worried I'm going to get in trouble that I squat down when I see head lights approaching.

"It's okay, it's just an oncoming car, don't worry."

"We'll go to Bradley's house tonight and get a good night's sleep, then tomorrow we start our adventure!" Faith tells me.

"So we're going to New Orleans?" I'm still a little afraid to go somewhere that Mama can't find me.

"I got a job there at a bank, it's a good paying job and it's far enough away that we won't have to worry about anyone finding us," my uncle says.

"Will I go to school?"

"Yes. We'll buy you some new clothes and you can start school after the holidays. What do you think your new best friend's name will be?" Faith asks.

"Hmm, I think it will be Julia. She'll have pudgy cheeks and lots of freckles, her hair will be red and she'll be really smart," I answer.

"I wonder who my best friend will be?" Faith asks.

"Why me of course," Bradley answers. He reaches across me to pat Faith's knees and she smiles at both of us.

Faith and Bradley help me make up the davenport for my bed. I am tired from a long day and fall to sleep easily. In the morning Bradley makes pancakes for breakfast and then we load the car with our belongings and hit the road.

"Where are we going to live?" I ask, suddenly curious.

"I rented a nice apartment in a house outside of town. It has two bedrooms, so you'll have your own space. The landlady said she has a pretty brass bed we can borrow, would you like that?"

"I would. Are we going to get a Christmas tree? Will there be a mantel for our stockings?"

"Of course, we'll get a tree this week if you'd like. Christmas is right around the corner so we better get a move on it. If we don't have a mantel we'll have to be creative, we could always hang our stockings on our stairs."

"Speaking of stockings, look what the ladies gave us as a parting gift." Auntie Faith opens the carpet bag she holds and pulls out three handknit stockings. Each one has our names stitched across the top and they all have different designs. My stocking has a Santa Claus with a fluffy white beard. Faith's has a

Christmas tree with bells sewn on, and Bradley's has a reindeer. How marvelous.

"They are so pretty. I can't wait to hang them!" I say clapping my hands together.

In less than three hours we arrive at our destination. The house has a gray stone front with black shutters and looks like a mansion. There is a covered front porch that stretches across the entire house and rocking chairs with pillows and lots of plants take up the space. The house has a center hallway that branches off into several apartments. Ours is on the left side in the front of the house. It's spacious and airy, the ceilings are high, and in fact we do have a fireplace and mantel to hang our stockings from.

"Auntie Faith, can I have the stockings?" I ask.

She hands them over to me and I hang them carefully from the nails that are already in place beside the grate. I stand back to admire them and am hit with a sudden longing for my family. We had a whole row of nine stockings across our fireplace. I miss my parents and my siblings, even my mean sister Sally, something fierce. I will pray every night that they find me here.

It doesn't take long for us to unpack our belongings. Auntie Faith and I don't have a lot of personal items, but Bradley has plenty of household things like pots and pans and lamps to get us started. The landlady gave us permission to use anything from the attic, and Faith allows me to go up and have a look around.

Silky spider webs hang from the eves of the wooden plank walls and a musty smell fills the air. There is a dingy wicker baby buggy and a Patsy Anne doll with blue eyes and mangled hair.

"Look what I found," I say showing Faith my treasure.

"A Patsy Ann doll? My goodness, I used to have one just like her! Mine didn't have real hair though, let's find out who she is," Faith says.

We lift up her dress and look for the dolls marking on the

back. Sure enough I have a Mary Ann doll from the Patsy Anne collection.

"I'm going to ask Santa Claus to bring me some material so that I can make her clothes! Maybe some doll furniture too," I say hugging my treasure.

"What a wonderful idea, I suppose you better work on a letter to him then, huh?"

Faith hands me some paper and a pen. I date the letter in the upper left hand corner and start my list.

Bradley surprises us later in the evening with a spectacular ten foot pine tree that fits perfectly in the parlor beside the bookcase.

There are hundreds, possibly thousands of books on these bookshelves! I could stay here forever and never read them all! I choose The Story of Doctor Doolittle by Hugh Lofting to be my first book.

We don't have any garlands for the tree so in the morning Auntie Faith and I go shopping for ornaments. We purchase a few yards of ribbon to tie into bows, some gingerbread men, and make a garland from cranberries and popcorn.

When the tree is decorated and Faith is in the kitchen cooking supper, I dive into my book holding my dolly by my side. I was worried about escaping, but I didn't need to be, because this is heaven.

CHAPTER 22

CHRISTMAS

On Christmas eve, Bradley, Auntie Faith and I go to mass at a new church. There is a nativity play and the girl playing Mary makes me giggle. She can't stop from laughing and her smile is so bright that I ask God to make her my friend. We sing Christmas carols and meet a few of the parishioners before going to our new home. I overhear Faith telling folks that we are from Jackson, but that we just moved here for Bradley's new job. I guess that's what I will tell people too.

I toss and turn all night long waiting for Santa to arrive, but I guess I fell asleep though. The rising sun peeking through my window wakes me, I jump from bed and run to wake up my family.

"Hurry!" I yell, anxious to see what Santa has left me.

My stocking is full to the brim with tiny wrapped gifts, there is even a tiny table and chair for my doll! I unwrap a few books, a new dress, lots of ribbons for my hair, and a shiny pair of shoes.

"Thank you!" I say to Faith and Bradley. I give them both big hugs and play with my gifts all morning long. I will start school in a few days but until then I intend to play.

Faith makes French toast for our breakfast with sausage links on the side. I eat every last bite and use my napkin to wipe my mouth. I want to use my best manners around my new family so they keep me. I even help clean up like a good girl when the meal is over.

Bradley is in the parlor enjoying a cigar and Auntie Faith is reading a new book. I decide to go back up to the attic to see what else I can find. I walk through a spider web and it gets tangled in my hair and clings to my clothes. When I try to peel it from me it sticks to my fingers.

I hear a scratching sound, it's soft but persistent. It's coming from beneath a large piece of furniture in the corner. When I step closer I realize there is something alive. I run downstairs for Faith and Bradley and they follow me cautiously back to the attic.

"Well I'll be darned, it's a litter of kittens," Faith says upon closer inspection.

"They can't be more than a few days old," Bradley adds.

"Where is the mama?" I ask.

"She must be around somewhere, she wouldn't leave them alone for long. We better keep our distance. Here you can sit across the room and keep an eye on things," Faith instructs positioning a chair against the wooden wall for me.

"Can I have one of the kittens?"

Auntie Faith and Bradley exchange smiles and tell me that they need to check with the landlady first, but if she says yes then I can. This is far and away the best Christmas I've ever had.

FAITH

CHAPTER 23

NEW ORLEANS

There isn't a fence standing between me and the outside world anymore. Nowadays I can go anywhere I'd like without worrying I'll be caught and reprimanded. It's liberating and daunting at the same time.

I am busy from sun up until sun down with all of my errands as well as the cooking and cleaning. At Carville so much was done for us, all of our meals were provided, we were granted our medical care as well as a place to live. Now Bradley and I have to make sure we can make ends meet, this means careful planning on my behalf and I find it can be stressful sometimes. I set aside money in an envelope for meals and clothing, toiletries, and items for the house. Luckily Jenny isn't a fussy eater and she doesn't want for much.

I've saved and scrimped so that Bradley and I can meet for lunch today at the D.H. Holmes department store. It's our three-month wedding anniversary and we have a reservation at Arnaud's. Bradley's co-workers have told him the Shrimp Arnaud, the house special, is sensational. My stomach has been off the past few days and I'm not sure I can eat a large meal, so I may just have fish stew or clam chowder. All of the fine food and no Sisters to watch over me and limit how much I eat is making my waist thicker. It's hard not to indulge because everything is so tempting.

Jenny and I often walk along Canal Street after school, if she is hungry we go to White Castle for a quick burger. The sandwich is made with Parker House rolls and they only cost twelve cents. We usually get soft drinks too and when we're good and full we cross the street to Solari's. Here we pick fresh fruits and vegetables to have at home for a simple supper.

Today there are a few shady characters walking around, but still New Orleans has to be the most exciting place I have ever lived. I haven't been to the French Quarter yet and would never venture there alone, but Bradley promises he'll take us there for an excursion soon.

"Hello, Joan," I say to the bank secretary who is always wearing the latest fashion trend. "I am here for Bradley."

"It's nice to see you, Faith. You look lovely today, why I'd even say you're glowing," Joan says.

"It must be all the fresh air," I suggest.

"Whatever you're doing, it's working. I'll tell Mr. Jackson that you're here."

"Thank you, I think I'll wait outside on the bench."

"Suit yourself," Joan says.

Hmm, I wonder why I am glowing, it's a peculiar thing to say to someone you hardly know. I've heard people say that to pregnant women...I can't be, we've only been married a short while. Could it happen that quickly? We make love nearly every night but the ladies from Carville assured me it took longer, sometimes a year, to get pregnant. Why, it took Marilyn longer than a year to become with child.

I'll post a letter to her today and ask what the symptoms are like. I don't feel any different at all, except that my clothes are tighter...but I thought that was from the variety of new foods I am enjoying to excess.

"There you are!" Bradley kisses me and spins me around.

He looks dapper in his suit coat and tie, dress slacks, and polished shoes. He wears his hair quite short now and while I miss his curls, it shows off his blue eyes.

"You made a reservation right, darling?" he asks.

"No, you were supposed to," I say.

"Uh oh,"

"Did you really forget?"

"No, I'm only teasing you. How could I forget our anniversary? I bought you a gift, here, hold out your arm."

I give him my right arm instinctively. He reaches into his pocket and withdraws an unusual looking piece of jewelry that he clasps on my wrist.

"It's a scarab bracelet, they're all the rage according to Joan," he laughs.

"It's certainly unique, I love all the colors, thank you!" I hug my thoughtful husband and even though I am tempted to ask where he got the money for such a lavish gift, I bite my tongue.

As soon as we enter Arnaud's I feel queasy. Normally I love seafood, but today the strong odor of scallops cooking permeates the air and turns my stomach.

"Are you okay?" Bradley asks me.

"I'm not sure," I answer honestly. "I feel fine, it's just the smells are making me nauseous. It's probably a stomach bug, nothing more."

"Let's not eat here then, I can't have you fainting on me during our meal," he says, escorting me from the restaurant.

"How about if we walk for a bit?" When we are back outside I put on my French beret.

"Sure, it's a nice enough day," he says.

"Bradley, do want a large family?" I ask catching him off guard.

"How large are we talking about?"

"Oh heck, I don't know. Two or three children?" I say. "Plus Jenny, that sounds perfect. My job is going swell and I'm planning to ask for a raise at my six-month assessment."

"I hope you get it; sit down," I say motioning for him to join me on a park bench.

"What is it? What's wrong?"

"I'm not sure, but I think I might be with child," I say waiting for his reaction.

Bradley jumps up from the bench and whoops and claps his hands. He lifts me in the air and spins me around, then gently places me on the ground.

"How do you know? How far along are you?" He's as happy as I've ever seen him.

"Everything smells funny to me and now that I think about it I've gained a few pounds. But it wasn't until Joan told me I was glowing that I started to wonder. I haven't had my monthlies for two cycles."

"Is that unusual for you? Is there anyone you can talk to about this? Have you made any friends you can confide in?" he wonders.

"I've met a few neighbors, but they're only acquaintances, Bradley. I've been busy I guess."

"Let's make an appointment with a female doctor at once," he insists.

"I'll try to get a few names and schedule something, but Bradley I'll be so fat." I remember my mother complaining about how fat she got when she was pregnant. She made the whole experience sound dreadful.

"Never mind about that, as long as you're healthy that's all that matters."

"What about the baby, what if he or she catches Hansen's disease from me? I'll have to tell the doctor that takes care of me, and surely he'll want me back at Carville."

"Dammit. We should have been more careful," he makes a fist with his hands.

"I'm sorry, I didn't think this would happen so soon," I admit.

"It's not your fault, there are things I should have done."

"Like what?"

"Pull and pray."

"I don't understand," I say.

"I should have pulled out from you before I let go, and then prayed. I'm sorry, Faith. Let's not tell anyone until we're certain you're carrying. We'll figure something out, we always do."

Bradley and I walk a little longer and drink coffee and eat sandwiches from the corner store for lunch. I walk him back to the bank and head for home. This is supposed to be the most exciting time in a woman's life, so why then am I suddenly petrified?

CHAPTER 24

WILLIAM

Rather than go directly home I stop in a women's clothing store to have a look at the maternity frocks. Nothing jumps out at me and I realize it's nearly time to get Jenny from school. When I leave the store and turn the corner, I bump smack into a gentleman whose nose is buried in a book.

"I'm terribly sorry," I say, reaching into my purse for napkins. I've spilled the man's coffee and it's soaking through his paperback.

"It's alright, I should have been paying attention. Frances?" the man asks after a pause.

It's been so long since I've heard my birth name that I hardly react. I realize the man is staring at me and waiting for my reply.

"No, my name is Faith, you must have me confused with someone," I say. I am terrified that the person connected with this familiar voice and face has recognized me.

"I'm certain I don't, I'd know you anywhere, Frances. I thought you were in New York?"

I study his face; I remember those lovely eyes. It is my dearest William.

"William? What on earth are you doing here?" I ask, my heart skipping a beat.

"What am I doing here, why I live here. I'm a partner in the Presley law firm, I have been for over a year now, how about you? Your sister told me you fell madly in love with a fellow in New York and she doubted you'd ever be back."

"Is that really what she said? I'm not surprised."

"You were in New York weren't you? You told me that

yourself."

"It's complicated, look, I need to be going, though it is nice to see you."

"Shall I tell Emily I bumped into you?"

I grab William's arm, "William, if you ever cared for me at all, I beg you not to tell Emily you saw me today,"

"I don't normally keep secrets from my fiancée, but if you insist," he agrees not to mention my name.

"I insist, and about those secrets, well never mind." I storm off to pick up Jenny from school, and when she runs to me my mind is elsewhere.

"Auntie, look!" she shows me her art project, it's a drawing of "Dotty," her kitten.

"What a lovely drawing, you got the shading just right," I say as we walk home hand in hand.

Jenny's so happy here, but if this is where William and Emily live I risk being discovered every single time I leave the house. Between this and the baby I am feeling doomed all over again.

CHAPTER 25

LIFELINE

I am indeed pregnant. I've started having morning sickness and can barely keep a meal down. Bradley is worried I will lose the baby, but I assure him this is normal. Or at least I've been told it's normal.

I don't want to see a doctor because anyone with a medical degree will recognize my symptoms of Hansen's disease immediately upon doing an exam. I've developed several pale patches of skin on the soft inner portion of my thighs that can't be disguised. Not to mention the fingers on my right hand, the pointer and index finger are slowly absorbing into my body. Dr. Jo described this strange phenomenon to me when I was a patient at Carville. I wear fashion gloves outdoors so no one notices, but if I wear the gloves inside a doctor's office it will be his first tip. I ran out of medication a month ago and that's when the patches appeared.

"What do we do, Bradley? Should I try to find a midwife?" I ask one night in bed.

"No, midwives are illiterate, dirty women with no real knowledge of babies, I won't allow it. Let me think…what if we cover your patches with make-up?"

"It won't work, it will only make them stand out more, I know because I've tried."

"Dammit to hell. They'll take you back to Carville in handcuffs and put you in the detention center, I can't have that."

"Even if I volunteer to go back they won't let me keep the baby there. I knew two women both who came to Carville pregnant but the minute the babies were born, they were taken away, they weren't even allowed to hold them," I say in distress.

"I can take care of the baby and Jenny too, we'll live right in Carville if we have to, I can find a job as a laborer," he says.

"Bradley, you're a banker now, I can hardly ask you to work as a laborer, that's not fair to you."

"The only thing that matters, darling, is that one of us takes care of our baby, and if that one of us is me, so be it."

"What if I am in huge trouble for escaping and for taking Jenny with me?"

"They can't prove you took her, you could say she followed you," Bradley suggests.

"I hate lying, I should just come clean if I have any wish to get back in Dr. Jo's good graces."

"They'll ask about Jenny, then, and want you to bring her with you when you return."

"I know."

"She's doing so well here, too. I haven't noticed any new patches, have you?"

"One, on her ear, her case appears to be mild but it's such a fickle disease that could change any moment." The scaly patch on Jenny's ear is right on her lobe, I've seen patients whose entire ears are covered with pustules and scabs.

"Let's sleep on it for a few nights, we don't have to make a decision this minute," my husband says.

When I close my eyes I think about William, I feel like I am betraying the man beside me. I don't lust for my old beau by any means, but seeing him today was jarring. It made me wonder about his life with Emily and whether or not they are happy. It also made me spitting mad at my sister for catching William with lies. Emily was always a self-absorbed young woman, but maybe now she has changed and softened. I hope that it's true, for William's sake at the very least.

I've thought about tracking William down at his office and

inquiring about Emily, but decide against it. Everyone will be better off if I leave well enough alone.

I am afraid to leave the house, Bradley thinks I am worried I'll be sick in public, but it's because I don't want to risk running into William or Emily. I still pick Jenny up from school and walk home with her, but we don't venture into the city limits anymore. Instead, I make up reasons I need to get home, today for instance there is a pie in the oven and I don't want it to burn.

"What kind of pie?" Jenny asks,

"Guess," I tell her. When we are nearing our home I notice a swarm of policemen on the front lawn.

Oh, my God. William confided in Emily and she tracked me down and turned me in. How could she do this to me again? Am I really that threatening to her?

"Jenny, listen, we need to talk. I know this is sudden, but I may have to go back to Carville." I lean down so that I am eye level with Jenny.

"Why, Auntie?" Jenny's lips tremble and she starts to cry.

"Well, the good news is that I'm having a baby! However, I think someone here may have discovered that I have Hansen's."

"Who? Your doctor?"

"No, I haven't met with any doctors yet, we were buying us some more time, dear, while we figured things out. I love you as if you were my own, and so does Bradley, but if I go back I'm afraid you'll have to come back too. I am afraid the folks at Carville won't rest until they have you, see they might think I kidnapped you. They could make things very difficult for me if I go alone."

"But you didn't! I wanted to go, I won't go back, I won't!" Jenny stomps her feet and makes a fuss. I wrap her in my arms and don't know what to do.

"Look. See those policemen at our house? I bet they are there for me. There won't be anyone to take care of you now, Bradley has to work and save money for our future and your mother is in Alabama."

I briefly think about handing the child over to my sister but realize the second she discovers her marks she'll turn her in anyway.

"I don't know what to do, Jenny, it seems we are in a pickle."

We walk hand in hand, chins up, to the house to meet the situation head on. When we cross the lawn a pair of officers approach us and ask me if I am Mrs. Faith Jackson. I put my arms out as if they'll be cuffed, instead the officers tell me to sit down on the porch.

"Ma'am, there has been an accident, I'm afraid your husband was killed at the scene."

"What?" I reposition my hands to my side then grab Jenny and hold her tightly. It's simply not possible.

"It was a car accident, I'm afraid he was hit head on. He was taken to the hospital and pronounced dead on arrival. I'm required to take you there to identify the body and sign some papers," the officer says, unable to meet my eyes.

Surprise steals my breath and shock takes over my body. I instinctively put my hand across my belly, there is a flutter, and I swear I am feeling the baby move for the first time.

The officer escorts Jenny and me into his vehicle. I can hardly breathe, I simply can't live without Bradley. He has become my life. I feel detached from the situation, like everything is happening around me and I am simply a bystander. I can't speak and my mind has gone numb.

"Mrs. Jackson," the officer who has been calling my name says, "we're here."

I walk on air, feeling no pressure beneath my feet, as if I'm boundless. My heart beats in my chest, words are mere echoes.

Jenny is still attached to me, my lifeline, my darling girl.

CHAPTER 26

EMILY

The morgue is cold and dark and smells like formaldehyde. One of the officers waits outside with Jenny while the other takes me in to identify Bradley's body. His corpse is lying on a steel cart, he is draped in a white sheet and there is a tag with his name dangling from his big toe. My love, the father of my child, nothing but a lifeless form taking up space now. I never asked him if he wanted to be buried or cremated.

The remainder of the afternoon is surreal. I haven't made any funeral arrangements and don't know where to begin. Joan has phoned twice to ask how she can help, but I don't know how anyone can help me now. Several of Jenny's friends from school have heard that her father died. One by one the moms come with casseroles and flowers.

The doorbell rings at six in the evening and I am nearly ready to put on my pajamas and collapse into bed. I expect the landlady to call so I answer the door and open it wide for her to come in. However, it's not the landlady but another young lady.

"Frances?" the woman says.

I am in a fog, but even in my detached state I recognize my sister.

"Oh no, was it your husband?" she asks, stepping back from the stairs knowing full well I am a leper.

"It was. You can't have a child Jenny's age, how did you find out?"

"You can't have a ten year old either."

"Her mother asked me to watch out for her…" is all I say.

"I am a nanny for Jenny's classmate Samantha. My employers asked me to bring you this," she says handing over a lasagna.

"Now that you know where I live I assume you'll be turning me in?"

"I don't know, I'm not sure."

"Please don't. Give us some time, we have to bury Bradley and figure out what to do; I'm with child," I admit, praying on my sister's sympathies.

"Frances, how could you? You're not even supposed to be outside of Carville, if anyone finds out they'll have you arrested."

"I fell in love. My case is so mild that we wanted to try to build a life, a normal life. We aren't hurting anyone, Emily."

"You are hurting anyone you come into contact with. You're a leper, Frances. Mother and Father told me I was never to write to you and that I would never see you again, it's a filthy disease and you don't belong here," she spit.

"Can you at least show a little humanity? I just lost my husband. I am responsible for Jenny and have this child to think about now," I say as I unconsciously rub my belly.

"You belong in Carville."

"They won't let me keep the baby there, Emily. What would you have me do?" I plead with my sister who is far more of a stranger than relative.

"What about Jenny? Is she a leper too?" Emily asks.

"Who's at the door, Auntie?" Jenny comes to the door holding her kitty and sees Emily.

"Hello, Miss," Jenny says.

"What did you say your name was, I'm sorry I am having trouble focusing just now," I say so that Jenny doesn't think I know the person at our door.

"I am the soon to be Mrs. Emily Cooper, I am betrothed, see?" Emily flashes her engagement ring and catches herself. She remembers she is in the presence of lepers and covers her mouth and nose at once as if we are vile, smelly creatures.

"This kind lady has brought us a meal, put it in the kitchen please, Jenny," I say handing her the dish. Jenny puts her kitten down and does as instructed.

"I have to go inside, Emily. It was nice to see you again," I say shutting the door behind me. I can't help but wonder how long it will be before the whole world knows we are dirty lepers now. Emily will twist this to fit her needs. Ever since we were children she was spiteful and jealous.

***

It surprises me that no police officers came to call on us last night and return us to Carville. Jenny and I dress in our best attire and walk to the funeral home where we will say goodbye to Bradley. The service is small, Joan sits in the back row of chairs and a few other people from Bradley's bank are there as well. The bank president sent a gorgeous bouquet of flowers and I feel honored that my husband was well regarded.

I ask Joan if she will keep an eye on Jenny for an hour. I have an errand to run and need to do it alone. William works for the Presley law firm, he said it was just up the street from where we bumped into each other. He may be my only hope now so I have to find him, no matter the cost.

***

"What on earth?" William says when the secretary shows me into his office.

"Frances, you look horrible, Cindy get her a glass of water please," he instructs his secretary.

"I need to talk to you. I don't have a lot of time, but first of all I want to tell you the truth and then I need a favor. William, I wasn't sent to New York to help my aunt and I didn't fall in love and get married in the city. I was sent to Carville, I have Hansen's disease. Now I've gone and got myself in trouble. My husband just passed away two days ago, he was killed in a car accident..." my voice catches and I stop speaking.

"I heard about the accident, but I didn't know that was your husband. I'm terribly sorry." William is at my side comforting me.

"I escaped Carville with a minor, a girl named Jenny. Her mother asked me to watch out for her and I couldn't leave her behind. Now I'm pregnant and not sure what to do. If I go back to Carville that means Jenny has to go back too, I don't have anyone to take care of her here. I won't be allowed to keep my baby and will have to put her in an orphanage. I don't know if I'll do jail time for kidnapping, or if it can be overlooked somehow. My case is mild, so is Jenny's. Bradley and I just wanted a normal life, we were in love. I nearly died at Carville; I volunteered for tests and it was awful..." I start to cry again and William hands me a handkerchief. I blot my nose and eyes and dare to look at him.

"I wish someone told me the truth years ago. I loved you. I would have married you anyway, to hell with everyone else."

"That's a nice thing to say, I loved you too. Emily sent me a letter that you had eyes for her all along and that you refused my letters when they came."

"What? That's simply not true. Emily is, well, let's just say she's not you. We're newly engaged and I'm not sure I can go through with the wedding. We're very different people, but that story can wait. What is it you need from me?"

"I need help finding someone."

"Okay, I can look into that, whom do you need to find?"

"I need to find Jenny's mother. She's living somewhere in Alabama, and William, I need a place to hide until I have the baby," I confide.

CHAPTER 27

HOLDING OUT

Jenny and I pack our things and leave the mansion in the middle of the night. William is waiting for us around the corner in his car and promises to take us somewhere safe while he searches for Jenny's mother. I didn't expect he'd bring us to his home but that's exactly what he does.

"I think you'll be comfortable here, please make yourself at home," he says. His house is plenty large enough to accommodate us, Jenny and I will share a room adjacent to his upstairs. We have a separate bathroom with a sink and claw foot tub.

"Are you sure you'll have us? The baby isn't due for six months. I don't want to put you out or ruin what you have with my sister, if she finds out…"

"She won't find out. I will make sure of that, and yes, I'm sure you can stay here. I will let my housekeeper know we have guests and I'll swear her to secrecy. Let me do this for you, please."

"Thank you, William. You're a good friend."

"I should have known Emily was lying to me years ago, can you forgive me?" he asks searching my eyes for grace.

"Of course I forgive you. I admit it was painful when I found out you were with my sister, but I had no choice but to move forward with my life. I just don't understand how Emily could be so cruel, and my parents…they've never reached out to me since I was diagnosed. They hate me, but none of this is my fault. I have a disease, but I didn't ask for it, it could just as easily have been one of them." I vent my frustration and anger to William who seems to understand my plight.

"I can't imagine what you're going through. I'm so sorry about your husband, what more can I do?" he asks genuinely, wanting to help.

"Having us here and helping me find Jenny's mother is all I can ask of you. I need to take care of Jenny first, then I need to find a place for my baby. They'll put her in Saint Elizabeth's orphanage if I don't find someone willing to adopt her. This is my child, my flesh and blood, I want her raised in a loving home." I can't keep my emotions in check and release all that's been bottled up since Bradley's accident.

"I'm going to help you through this, Frances. You are not alone." Frances hardly feels like it belongs to me anymore so I ask him to call me Faith from now on.

"Why aren't you afraid of us like everyone else?"

"Maybe I should be, but we've kissed many times and I have no symptoms. I am healthy. I firmly believe God has kept me this way and put you in my path so I can help you now when you need it most. I will hire a private investigator to help find Jenny's mother, it will all be okay. I promise."

Jenny and I unpack our suitcases into the dressers in the spare room. There are twin beds and two side tables for our things. Jenny has already claimed the far bed and has her dolls positioned on the fluffy pillows. I need to locate her mother quickly, and pray her father agrees to my plan. What I am about to ask is no small favor.

I have a restless sleep and feel unwell when I wake up. My morning sickness is draining me and the housekeeper wants me to see a doctor at once. When I tell her that's not possible she makes some inquiries on my behalf and at half past noon a midwife shows up at the door carrying a satchel full of odd looking instruments.

"How far along are you?" The midwife named Susan asks. Bradley said midwives were dirty and uneducated, but Susan is perfectly pressed and well groomed. Her fingernails are short and clean and her hair is in a tidy bun at the nape of her neck.

"I can't say for certain, maybe eight weeks?"

"Your morning sickness will get better in the second trimester, lay back and let me have a look at you. Take off your top so I can feel your belly."

Susan presses on my belly with cold hands, she doesn't ask me to spread my legs so my patches go unnoticed for the time being.

"You're farther along than you thought, twelve weeks on the nose. I'm surprised your morning sickness is just starting now. The wee one is healthy, but you on the other hand; I know why won't see a real doctor. I've seen it before."

Susan doesn't use the term leprosy or Hansen's disease, she simply lifts my hands into her own and stares at my mottled fingers. "You're lucky, it's been kind to you. I've seen far worse."

"So have I. I will go back to Carville as soon as I have the child, I just need to see her when she is born. I won't hold her, but I need to see her."

"I understand, have you found someone to take her yet?"

"I'm working on that," I say.

"The child with you, Jenny, is it? She has a patch on her left ear, she shouldn't be in school," Susan warns.

"I know, we ran out of medicine and the patches appeared. I'll keep her here with me until we find her mother."

I spend the morning resting and Jenny helps the housekeeper in the kitchen. At five o'clock the supper table is set and I expect William to come through the door any second. The door opens and Emily flies in, "William, you'll never believe it...William?" Emily shouts.

I freeze in my position at the table, Emily is in the front hallway taking off her coat and scarf, ready to barge in.

"Miss Emily, William is not at home at present. He asked me to tell you he'll be out of town for a few days, he'll get in touch with you upon his return."

"But I have urgent news that can't wait, where is he, I'll ring him," Emily says.

"He doesn't tell me where he is going, but the message was clear, he'll phone you when he returns."

"Why do I smell roast beef then? If William isn't here who are you cooking for? Are you taking advantage of him? Why you insolent..." she went on to berate, Mrs. Fox, the help.

"I'd never...he gave me permission to use the kitchen for guests, Miss."

"I better have a look..." she says and walks into the dining room to find the table expertly set.

"You!" Emily says when she sees me.

"Hello Emily," I say, a slow, burning hatred builds in my heart.

"You need to leave right now, if William knew you were a dirty leper he'd throw you out. How dare you..." she rants.

"I invited her to stay with me, Emily. Kindly refrain from using that term in my home. It's derogatory and hurtful." William has come home in time to witness the scene.

"But William, she is contagious, she belongs in a leper home. How could you do this to me?"

"Emily, this isn't about you, it's about helping someone I care for," his cold glare can't hide his anger.

"I see, very well then, William." Emily storms out of the house, slamming the door behind her.

"She's going straight to the police, I can guarantee it," I say.

"You're probably right. I can ask around, see if anyone has a few rooms for you and Jenny."

"No, I can't do that to anyone else. We'll pack our things and leave tonight, I don't want to cause you anymore trouble than I already have."

"Where will you go?"

"There's only one place we can go, back to Carville," I say reluctantly.

"At the very least let me make some calls for you, I can talk to the doctor and brief him on your situation. Maybe it will help smooth the transition, I hate the thought of you in jail, even at Carville."

"It's a small jail, or detention center, but it's uncomfortable or so I've heard. There are enough rumors to know I don't want to spend anytime there," I admit.

"Consider it done. I'll find Jenny's mother, we'll take care of your baby, don't worry, Faith." William holds me close, his body pressing against mine holding me the way someone would hold a lover.

"We'll be out of your hair by tomorrow morning," I promise.

In the morning while we pack our belongings once again, the police arrive as I expected. Emily wasted no time turning us in and stands on the sidewalk now to make sure we are cuffed and removed.

I was arrested for kidnapping a minor and for public endangerment. The cuffs feel tight on my wrists but the pain can't match what I see in Jenny's eyes, she is heart broken that we are going back to Carville.

JENNY

CHAPTER 28

CARVILLE ONCE MORE

When we arrive back at Carville Auntie Faith is brought under the law and forced to serve several weeks in the clink regardless of her pregnancy. It is a light sentence considering she took me with her, but we stick to the story we concocted and say I followed her without her knowing. I am assigned a new room in the dormitories far away from her. We fought to be together but it was a battle we lost. Not even William could change Dr. Jo's mind on this subject.

It has taken a few days but now everything is back to normal for me. The only thing I really miss is my kitty, Dotty, but William is going to take care of her.

Dorothy is irate that I didn't tell her I was escaping. She gave me the silent treatment for a week, but when I gave her one of my dolls she warmed up and we went back to being best friends. Dorothy has gotten worse while I was away. Her eyes have a thick milky crust now and I can tell she has even more pain in her feet. She can't apply any pressure to them anymore and has to rely on help to get anywhere.

When Auntie was released from the clink she was placed in a new cottage with women she doesn't know. We both miss Bradley, but for Auntie the pain is unbearable. I remember how I felt when I lost Daniel and remember that she saved me from my grief. Auntie Faith started swimming again at night when she was released from detention. She sneaks out through the hole in the fence that Bradley swore he was going to mend but never did.

I often follow her to the water to make sure she comes back. Sometimes I swim with her, but usually I just watch. Auntie's graceful strokes are mesmerizing, she glides across the water, her large belly hugged by the soft ripples she creates. She is due any day now and I think this is the only place she truly feels at peace with herself. She has lost too much and it's up to me to bring her back.

***

Auntie Faith gave birth to a healthy baby girl in the middle of the night. She weighs six pounds and seven ounces and is nineteen inches long. As soon as she was born, she was cleaned and swaddled in a soft pink receiving blanket and then removed from the birthing room and taken to the nursery immediately. Auntie wasn't allowed to hold her baby even once, but the kind nurse let her get a long look at her and she was able to memorize her little girl's sweet face. The baby has gray eyes, pudgy cheeks, and light brown wisps of hair; she resembles Bradley I am told.

Auntie has named the baby 'Hope'.

"All we need now is love," she says wistfully to me a few days later.

Hope will stay in the nursery until my mother arrives to bring her home. William hired a private investigator who tracked my mama down, finding her in Mobile, Alabama, where she was working as a secretary for a small business. My father is doing odd jobs when he can get them and we understand that money is tight. Sister Catherine says we are coming out of an awful depression and people are still grateful for any work they can get their hands on.

Caring for Hope adds to my family's financial burden but Faith promises to help as much as she can. Before she delivered the baby she started working in the records office where she earns a small paycheck. She saves every penny for her daughter and intends to send her wages directly to my family on a monthly basis. My mother promises to care for the baby and raise her as her own.

"Please tell her about me, and about Jenny," Faith says to my mother while the arrangements are being made.

"It's the least I can do for you, Faith. You are taking care of my daughter inside the fence, and I will take care of yours outside." My mother is kind and sympathetic, she understands better than anyone the heartbreak Faith is feeling.

CHAPTER 29

FALL FESTIVAL

The sweltering long summer days are finally behind us now that the seasons are changing. September is marked with falling temperatures over the course of the month. It will still be warm in the afternoon sun, but our clothes won't stick to us anymore and make us stinky when we work in the garden. It's time to plant seeds of bell peppers, eggplant, and tomatoes to harvest next year. The gardening group at Carville outlines the vegetable patch using Coca Cola bottles turned upside down and buried to the base. The company refuses to take our recyclable glass because we are lepers, so we use the bottles to divide the rows of vegetables and also to decorate the garden.

We harvest pumpkins from our patch and give them to the boys for carving. We decorate the dining hall with corn stalks, mums, and gourds and everything looks festive.

Next week Carville hosts its second annual fall festival complete with gumbo, shrimp, sugar cane, meat pies, and barbecue. The field workers are even cutting a maze into the cornfield so the children can wander through during the event.

***

When the day for the festival arrives, picnic tables are set up across the lawn and buckets of ice filled with Coca Cola line the pathway and are free for everyone to enjoy. There is a parade along River Road for the small children who dress up in the masks they made in school, using feathers and anything else they found to decorate them. Dr. Jo and his staff will be arriving on a float and will even be throwing candy.

I've heard there will be softball games all afternoon as well as three-legged races, an egg toss, bobbing for apples, and horseshoes. Prizes from the Canteen will be awarded to the top three winners in all categories.

Everyone is giddy, especially the single ladies, because the event is coed which is unusual here. All morning long the kitchen staff instructs us girls to husk corn on the cob while they prepare the vats of clarified butter and cornbread. Apples are sliced thin for pies and the extra bushels are saved for games.

Even Faith seems to be enjoying herself today. I stick close to her side and pull her away from the crowd towards a group of boys racing frogs. Several of the men went out into the lake last night and captured the creatures in sacks for the race. There are fat bullfrogs that refuse to budge and slimy green toads that leap out of the circle that cages them and into the lawn toward their freedom.

In the evening the adults drink whiskey and gamble using fake money the boys made earlier in the week. They play Bingo, Blackjack, and Roulette until all hours of the night. Everyone is happy and forgets any woes for the time being.

At some point Faith slips away from the fun and walks down to the water. I knew I'd find her there, in her special quiet place.

"Hi there," I say.

"Why aren't you enjoying the party?"

"Why aren't you?"

"I was feeling overwhelmed suddenly. I miss Bradley. My heart aches for Hope and sometimes I just need to be alone," she admits.

"Do you want me to leave?" I wonder out loud.

"No, you are always welcome by my side, without you I'd really be alone. I love you, you know that right? "

"I love you too, are you nervous about tomorrow?" I ask in

anticipation of the big day.

"I'm mostly excited, and a little nervous. What if she doesn't respond to me, what if she cries?"

"She won't, you'll see."

The full moon illuminates the river tonight as we sit side by side. Each of us lost in our own thoughts. When I yawn, Faith insists it's time to go to bed. She walks me to the dormitories and kisses me goodnight, I hug her tight and tell her to sleep well. Tomorrow is sure to be emotional, tomorrow my mother is coming to visit and she is bringing Hope with her.

CHAPTER 30

HOPE

Hope is six months old now and today we get to see her for the first time since she was born.

Auntie Faith does her best not to act anxious this morning, but I know she is nervous and overwhelmed. We both are. Auntie is so melancholy these days that I pray seeing her daughter will pull her from her doldrums.

"There they are!" I yell when I see my mother and the baby approaching the fence. My mother carries the baby in a sling and has a picnic basket with her, as always, that's full of goodies.

"Oh my, she is so big," Faith says.

"Mama," I yell, clutching the fence, waiting for my mother's touch. Faith stands behind me with her hands on my shoulders.

The baby is sleepy and ornery because she is hungry, but my mother says normally she has the disposition of an angel. We sit cross-legged on the ground, the fence is the only thing that separates us. My mother feeds Hope and we stare at the baby in wonder. It's obvious the baby looks just like Bradley, her hair is curly and her eyes are now a startling blue color. She sleeps through the night and only fusses when she needs a diaper change or to be fed.

"The money helps, thank you, Faith. I am able to stay home with her now all day because of the wages you send," my mother says to Faith.

"She's beautiful," Faith says, her eyes are full of tears and I know she longs to reach through the fence and touch her baby but she loves her enough not to.

"Mama, how is everyone at home?" I ask wondering about my sister, Sally, and my brothers Joey, Michael, Nolan, and Sam.

"Everyone is fine, we all miss you though."

"I miss you too, I made this for you in art class." I roll up my sketch of the boats sailing on the Mississippi River and hand it through the fence.

"You're becoming a fine artist, I'll hang it up in the foyer, if your dad allows."

"I'd like to go to college and become an art teacher one day," I say. I see my mother exchange a worried glance with Faith, they are afraid I'll get my hopes up.

"That's a lovely idea but," my mother starts to say.

"Mama, people are going to college nowadays right here at Carville!" I interrupt.

"Is that so?" she asks.

"It is true, a gentleman earned a business degree last month, it was a great cause for celebration wasn't it, Jenny?" Faith says, giving me a squeeze.

The baby's eyes are open now and she sits upright on my mother's lap. I feel a jealous pang that she gets to feel my mother's arms, while I am stuck over here. I long for my mother and Faith longs for her child, but circumstances prevent the union so we cling to one another instead.

Buntings, woodpeckers, red birds, and field larks flutter about building nests for the winter months ahead. Hope is alert and active as she watches the birds. When my mother lays her down on the blanket she grabs for her toes and brings them to her mouth for a nibble, which makes us all laugh. Her smile is heart warming and uplifting.

"How can we be sad when she is so happy?" I wonder out loud.

"That's a fair point, Jenny. You are wise beyond your years, do you know that?" Faith asks me.

"I've brought you some books, Jenny. When you finish them you can donate them to your library. How is it coming along?"

"The library has several thousand books now for everyone to enjoy. There is an amusement hall with a reading room too, so people can check out books and have a quiet place to read them," Faith explains.

"Wonderful, how else are you filling your time?"

"School, church, gardening," I say.

"Work, swimming, sleeping," Faith answers honestly.

"At least you have each other. I am grateful everyday for that."

After a few hours spent visiting on the lawn, the baby fusses and my mother says it's time for her nap. She'll be traveling home by train making it a very long day for them. We say our goodbyes and watch the pair leave. The scent of jasmine fills the air and mist rises from the water inviting us to swim.

"I'll race you!" Faith says to me, she's already undressing down to her skivvies and preparing to dive in, head first. I pull my knees to my chest and do a cannonball into the water, splashing Faith. She splashes me back and we both smile and feel happy now.

"You know what they say, don't you?" Faith asks me with a grin.

"What?"

"When life gives you lemons," and I chime in and repeat with her, "you make lemonade."

FAITH

CHAPTER 31

FAITH 1945

It's 1945 which means I've been living here at Carville for ten years. During my time here so much has evolved. The facility has gone from a cold inhospitable institution with sixty-five rooms to a well run community with one hundred buildings accommodating over three hundred and sixty-nine patients.

The facility has a progressive dairy with over two hundred cows, all of the milk is kept in-house and used to make ice cream, cheese, and yogurt. Carville cheese is among the best I've tasted to this day. We have our very own water tower for the laundry, there is a newly constructed power plant that supplies us with electricity, and we even have our own onsite electrician! Granted he still washes his money on payday and hangs it on the line to dry before leaving so he doesn't catch our germs.

We have a physical therapy building, a morgue, a Lion's Club for the men, numerous clubs for women, and the library has a collection of over ten thousand books. There is married housing now, docks by the lake for everyone to use, and there is even a Mexican program that teaches English to Spanish speaking individuals due to the large influx of the population. Perhaps best of all is that we now have an accredited school for the children.

***

Four years ago, Dr. Guy Faget became the new director for the National Leprosarium. He started a clinical trial using new drugs called sulfones, namely, Promin. He suspected this particular type of medication would prove to be the most promising treatment for Hansen's disease to date. Patients lined up to volunteer for the trial, myself included, because we would do anything to stop treatment with chaulmoogra oil. The doctor also experimented with different kinds of sulfone drugs, namely Diasone and Promazole. He also tried a cocktail of Dapsone, Rifadin, and Thiridozine. These were used to replace the chaulmoogra oil that had become the most common treatment for all patients even though it made the vast majority of us sick. Patients did have adverse reactions, such as irregular heartbeats and allergic reactions, to the new cocktail of drugs, but they were offset with Thalidomide.

By 1942 the beneficial effects of Promin were reported in leading medical journals across the nation such as, Public Health Reports and The Journal of American Medical Association. Promin proved to reverse symptoms for many patients. Ulcer lesions disappeared, and inflammation of the eyes and throat completely dissipated. Some thought it was a miracle and as a result, morale rose and folks were happy on campus. Children rode their bikes and roller skated from building to building through the corridors and in general a sense of well being was felt here at the hospital. There was even a rumor that any patient with clear labs for twelve months in a row would be able to go home.

In 1943, just two years ago, the first patients with clear smears for twelve months in a row were discharged. They were met with some resistance by the outside world, for instance they weren't allowed to ride the bus and were instructed to fumigate their clothes and purchase all new articles before entering town limits. This challenged many of the newly released patients because a large percentage of them had been abandoned by family, therefore they had no means to support themselves. Many of them came back to Carville as a result.

It wasn't until last year that Jenny and I were finally granted permission to live together in a sweet little cottage on Cottage

Row. Our home is furnished with seconds the nuns were able to find on their trips to town, the rest we made ourselves or received as gifts. Jenny is a skilled artist and her work adorns our walls and brightens the place up. We have curtains in bold colors on all the windows, our sofa has plump pillows, and there is a soft braided rug for our feet to land. Our kitchen is stocked with pots, pans, dishes, spices, pantry items, and anything else we need. I could never ask for more, we are lucky.

Time flies by and Jenny and I both remain in good health when compared to so many others afflicted here. It's both a blessing and a curse. It's a blessing that we don't have to endure any painful procedures such as amputations but when you look as normal as we do, it makes us long for the outside world even more.

Jenny is a young woman now and works with the children everyday, she is an excellent teacher and we both feel the good Lord called her here for this reason. I am spending the majority of my time working in the rehabilitation center. However, if I am needed in the dental clinic or the eye clinic, I happily fill in. I have yet to work in the pharmacy because titrating medications is a complicated task that requires expertise.

I have my meeting with Dr. Jo this afternoon and am hopeful my results are in. I had my smears done two weeks ago and my results have been negative for six months in a row now. Jenny's have been negative for three months. I am afraid to get my hopes up, but if in fact I am negative for Hansen's, I am going to put in a request for a day pass. Even one day on the outside would do me a world of good. A few women in my previous cottage were granted permission to leave the facility for a day or more. They had to write each town they would be passing through, detailing their circumstance and asking for written permission to be there. Some cases were granted and some weren't.

My sister Emily has publicly disowned me, and she vows never to speak to William again, which is fine by him. He and I have become dear friends, he is aware I will be putting in for a day pass and has offered to pick me up and take me wherever my heart desires. He'll even drive me to Mobile to see my daughter if I am given more than one day. He has never found anyone to marry and remains single. I detect he wishes our relationship amounted to more than friendship, but given our situation it's just not possible.

"Hello, Doctor," I say when I am called from the waiting room to the doctor's office.

"Faith, you look well. How do you feel?" he asks.

"I feel better than ever if I'm being honest. I don't have any patches. My skin is clear," I say hopefully.

"Well that matches your test results. You're clear again this month."

"Really?"

"Truly, the new medications are helping you keep the disease at bay. I personally grant you permission to take a short leave, no more than three days. I am not sure if you're aware but the American Public Health Association has just advised not to isolate lepers," he says.

"What does that mean? Do we all get to go home?"

"No, not yet. It just means they are catching on to my way of thinking that most people have a natural immunity to leprosy and that it's only mildly contagious to the rest. The common thought many doctors have now is that only open, infectious, cases require hospitalization. It's not unanimous, however, so for now everyone remains on campus. To me, this is a huge step in a promising direction. You may get out of here yet."

"Now that you mention it, have any of the doctors or staff ever contracted the disease?" I asked, curious.

"No, not one. Leading me to believe that ninety-five percent of us are immune."

"It's certainly encouraging, doctor. To think I could get out of here someday and live with my daughter, that's all I could ever ask for. I am not sure how I would support myself given that I am a single woman with little real life experience, that part is unsettling, but I will figure out a way to make it work."

"Yes, that's a problem for many patients here. Especially the elderly, some have been here nearly all their lives, this is their home."

"Jenny's grown up here, it's her home now too. Are her results in yet?"

"No, but I expect them in a few days."

"Very well, I'll put in my request for a three-day pass with each township I need to pass through to get to Mobile."

"If there's anything I can do to help, let me know," he says, giving me a hug before I let myself out of the room.

I ring William with the good news and he offers to post my letters to save me time and money. I will write to each township, including my letter of approval from the hospital, and he will be sure they are delivered by first class mail. I cross my fingers they grant me passage so that I can see Hope and spend time with William. It's a long drive, five hours, but the time spent together will be well worth it.

I am reluctant to tell Jenny my news because I don't want her to feel sad, but she knows me so well that she guesses before I even have time to explain.

"You're clear, I can tell. You're smiling from ear to ear."

"I've been granted a three-day pass!"

"That's the best news I've heard in a long time, I'm so happy for you," she appears to be genuine.

"Are you sure?"

"Of course I'm sure, I hope you get to see my family, and spend time with William," she looks at me with raised eyebrows. Perhaps I haven't been hiding my growing feelings for William as well as I thought.

"I look forward to that too, anytime with him is better than no time, I suppose."

"Hope is nearly same age now that I was when you and I first met…"

"Just about. Goodness, you were full of spit and vinegar when I first met you, do you remember? You were going to swim across the river and run away!"

"I remember, I probably would have died if it weren't for you, thank you."

"Don't thank me. Anyone would have done the same. I think we met that day for a reason, I don't know what I would have done all these years without you."

Jenny smiles and hugs me. She's become my daughter, my niece, and my little sister here inside the fence.

"Are you up for a tennis match?" I ask.

"I sure am, but let me get Dorothy so she can watch and keep score."

"I'll meet you on the court in let's say a half an hour?"

"Perfect," she says.

Poor Dorothy, the years have not been good to her. Jenny remains as faithful a companion to her friend as ever. Dorothy has lost her eyesight and ability to get around without help. She relies heavily on Jenny who is compassionate and considerate enough to oblige her every need. I am proud of the young woman I have helped to raise.

CHAPTER 32

OUTSIDE THE FENCE

I was granted permission to pass through all of the major cities from Carville, Louisiana to Mobile, Alabama. Luckily the cities along the way are enlightened and believe that Hansen's disease is not contagious as previously thought.

I prepare for my departure and have butterflies when the gate is opened and William is waiting for me in his shiny new Buick. He immediately comes towards me and takes my luggage. He pecks my cheek with a friendly kiss and opens the passenger side door for me. I wave goodbye to Jenny who is there to see me off. I can't help it but a feeling of guilt consumes me.

"Free at last," he says.

"It's a little strange, I'm not even sure how to behave on the outside, I feel guilty for my good fortune," I admit.

"No one will know anything about you, just act normal. Darling, you deserve this. Chin up now." William is encouraging and kind and I promise to enjoy this precious time.

"I wish Jenny could come too," I say.

"She'll just have to come along the next time, for now it's you and me, darling."

"Can we stop and get a little something for Hope along the way?" I ask.

"Of course, Jackson is the halfway point. We can get lunch and do some shopping, okay?"

"Lunch, in a restaurant?" I ask.

"Of course in a restaurant, you've been cleared, my dear, and I intend to treat you like a queen," he says.

"Oh boy, I like the sound of that, it's been a long time since I've been pampered."

"You deserve it, I mean it. You do."

"Why are you so good to me?"

"Why do you think?" he asks throwing the question back in my lap.

"I don't know, but I am grateful for your friendship."

"Is that what we are then? Friends?"

William is waiting for my reply and I debate whether or not to be honest with him about my feelings.

"I care about you, you know that. But if I am stuck in Carville the rest of my life, what do my feelings matter?"

"So you have feelings, then?" he pries.

"Yes, I do," I admit reluctantly.

William reaches across the seat and holds my hand, happy as a clam that I've admitted we're more than friends. There is an electric current charging the air, my body feels stimulated and excited all at the same time. William puts his blinker on and pulls the car over.

"What are you doing? Is there a problem?"

He leans in and kisses me. "There is no problem, it's just that I've been wanting to do that for years," he grins.

"Do it again, you have lost time to make up for," I tease.

We neck like school kids in the back seat of the car on the side of the road. Sexual tension fills the space between us and William opens the door and gets out of the car to walk it off.

"Something wrong?" I ask.

"Yes, I won't have you like this, God knows I want you, but it would be wrong."

"William, I'm no virgin and I'm certainly not a prude. I cast propriety aside a long time ago."

"I understand, but I want it to be different for us. I want it to be special," he says.

"It will be then, when the time is right," I say. We slide back into the front seat and continue on to Jackson.

When we arrive in the city I feel slightly overwhelmed by the crowds at the restaurant. I hide my hands in my lap so no one notices my fingers. The place is loud and full of life, I don't know whether to laugh or cry. I am so unused to being around large groups that it's overstimulating. Thankfully William orders for me and I have time to excuse myself and use the restroom before our meal arrives.

I study my face in the mirror. My features are delicate and symmetrical. I have crow's feet, a high forehead, and thin lips. Bradley and William have both told me I am beautiful, I can't say I believe that's true, but I am not ugly either. I have gained weight so I no longer look gaunt and rail thin. Some might even say I have a nice shape.

The service at the restaurant is stellar and the gumbo arrives within minutes of our order.

"I've missed this. The food at Carville is not bad, but this is delicious," I moan, leaning over my bowl.

I drain my bowl and soft drink and feel good and satiated. Now it's time to find something special for my daughter. There is a toy store and a bookstore on the main street, clothing shops, and yarn barns are just around the corner. I decide on a small doll from the toy store, and book from the bookstore. Jenny loved to play with dolls when she was ten and she was an avid reader, I realize that not all children like the same things but I'm satisfied with my purchase and have the shopkeepers wrap them separately with colorful paper and ribbon. I buy Jane and her family a box of chocolates to share and William buys a few cigars.

"We're almost there, are you doing okay?"

"I'm nervous, I guess. I don't know how she'll react to me. I've dreamed about this moment for so long and in my dreams Hope comes sailing into my arms and never lets go. She calls me 'mommy' and begs me never to leave. The reality is that I've only seen her once every year so, William, she hardly knows me."

"You write to her though, surely that counts for something, I think you're being silly. She will love you, just relax and be yourself," he advises.

When we arrive at Jane's home we are both pleased that it is in a nice part of town, far away from the derelict homes and ramshackle buildings. Jane comes out to meet us but Hope stays back and watches us through the window. The other children are either at school or work.

"Welcome, Faith. You must be William, it's a pleasure to meet you."

"The pleasure is mine, Jane." William says politely.

"Are you hungry? I've made some iced tea and lemon fingers."

"Sounds scrumptious," although I am still full from lunch.

"Hope, come here, darling. Come say hello to Faith."

She doesn't say, come say hello to your "mother", as I thought she might. The child is small and frail. I immediately sense that she is painfully shy. She climbs on Jane's lap and hides her eyes. She has wildly curly hair that can't be contained and Jane brushes it out of her eyes.

"Hope, remember I told you your mother was coming today? Surely you remember her, why it was only last Christmas that we paid her a visit," she reminds the child.

"It must be strange to see me without a fence between us. Hello, Hope. It's lovely to see you," I say gently, wishing my daughter would come to me.

Jane puts Hope down in the sturdy captain chair and pours our tea into tall glasses already filled with ice. She serves everyone her lemon fingers that have been dusted with confectioner's sugar. Hope eats hers in teeny bites, no wonder she is so small. She is beautiful; she has her father's eyes and my slight nose and lips. It is obvious she is well loved and that makes me happy.

I don't know what to say so I reach into my bag and offer Hope the gifts I've brought for her. Before she opens them she looks to Jane for permission. When Jane nods, Hope unwraps the doll, she looks happy and says a polite thank you. She is less excited about the book, but I tell her it was my favorite when I was a little girl.

"Jenny sends her love, she has been clear for several months now. She hasn't had symptoms for even longer. I hope the next time I visit she'll be with me. She's teaching now, she has a gift with children," I tell Jane who looks proud. I describe our small home and tell her about the new advancements at Carville.

"So people are being sent home?" she asks.

"A few, yes. It sounds like a dream come true, but for most of them it's been challenging. A few elderly folks were sent home but had no way to support themselves, their families wouldn't take them back and in the end they returned to Carville of there own volition. It's a growing concern for the staff at Carville and they are working on resolutions. They've established an ethics committee to help place anyone in need. The younger patients who work and have learned skills will do fine in the outside world, it's the middle aged and older population that's concerning."

"What about you? How will you support yourself when you are released?"

"I haven't gotten that far yet." Inwardly I was thinking it wouldn't just be myself that I'd have to support. I prayed Hope would want to live with me as well.

"Shall we take a walk and stretch our legs?" William suggests, "I'm feeling a little cramped in my thighs from the long drive."

Hope is quiet around me and our reunion is awkward and filled with clumsy, silent pauses. My daughter is perfectly cordial when she dares to speak, but to her I am a stranger.

When William and I leave the home to check into our hotel, I have an epiphany that brings me to my knees. It's true that I am Hope's birth mother, but Jane is her "mama", who she loves dearly.

William cradles me in his arms and takes me to bed. He tucks me in and turns off the light before heading to his adjoining room. I wake a few hours later and sneak into his bed, I need to be touched and loved. We fall into a natural rhythm with one another and he loves me in a way that makes me forget my woes and makes me feel alive.

CHAPTER 33

FREE TIME

I spend my free time thinking about William. We write letters and talk on the phone regularly professing our growing love and desire to be together.

In the meantime, I'm waiting patiently to hear whether or not Jenny's most recent study of bacteria is clean. She has tested clean for five months in a row and if today's results are negative it will be a great cause for celebration.

"Auntie!" Jenny yells as she runs towards me.

"Did you get your results?"

"Yes, I am clean again!" she says jumping up and down.

"Congratulations! Did they give you a day pass?"

"It's right here," she says showing me her pass. "I want to go into town and shop for a new dress, will you come?" she asks. She earns a nice wage as a teacher and is very frugal. I suspect she has someone she wants to impress but she hasn't admitted this to me yet so I don't bring it up.

"Of course, let's go tomorrow," I suggest.

In the morning we phone a cab and head into town. Jenny makes everything fun, she is light-hearted and kind, easy to talk to, and charismatic. She is so different from my own daughter, yet I feel closer to her than anyone else I know, except for William. William is my lover, Jenny is my closest companion.

We laugh over lunch and try on several ensembles until Jenny finds the one she falls in love with.

"I've met someone," she confides.

"I wondered."

"He's dreamy. He works at Carville, like Bradley used to…," there is a pause whenever one of us mentions Bradley's name.

"I'm happy for you, what's his name?" I ask wondering if I know the young man.

"His name is Michael. He works in the dairy, he brings the children ice cream every week and the moment I first saw him I was smitten."

"Have you been able to spend some time with him outside of the classroom?"

"A little, not as much as I'd like. Is that too forward?" she wants to know.

"Not at all, listen, you deserve all the happiness in the world. There's a dance next week, will he join you?"

"I don't know, we were thinking of a picnic along the lake. He likes to go fishing and offered to teach me."

"That will be a hoot, I can't imagine you baiting a hook with a worm!"

"I'll leave that part to him, I'm sure."

"Well, the outfit you've chosen will be perfect for the occasion. It's not too dressy or low cut. It's perfect, and the blush color suits your skin tone beautifully." I've raised a confident young lady who is becoming a woman before my very own eyes.

"I love you, have I told you that lately?"

"Only everyday," she laughs.

When I tell Jenny how terribly my reunion went with Hope she is beside herself. Imagining my pain was more than she could handle so she goes out of her way now to show me love, it is in the little gestures. It is in the extra cookie for dessert, or when she makes me a mug of tea 'just because'. She is never stingy with her hugs and affection and it is one of the things I admire about her most. Too many people here at Carville are guarded and afraid to love. Not Jenny, she wears her heart on her sleeve and she doesn't care who knows it.

CHAPTER 34

KEEPING SECRETS

It's 1946 and finally we've been given back the right to vote. It is a real triumph for my good friend Stanley who advocates tirelessly for our basic human rights to be restored. Stanley is a fearless activist who has achieved both social and legal breakthroughs as a result of his work at the newspaper that has been renamed, "The Star". Patients now have the right to use a telephone, they can write letters home, and now their voices can be heard when it comes to politics. Stanley spreads the word in his daily paper that leprosy is far less infectious than sexually transmitted diseases, or Tuberculosis. He works against the emasculation of the ego, as he refers to the injustices we face, caged within a metal barbed wire fence.

He is completely blind now, but even that doesn't deter him on his conquests to educate the public and remove the derogatory stigma of Hansen's disease. He continues to fight for reforms so that no one with Hansen's will be ostracized. Now that Promin is proving effective, he believes victims should be allowed to go home and, furthermore, that they should be treated with dignity. I admire my friend for his audacity and spirit, he never gives up in his fight to bring understanding and tolerance to the disease.

This news of Promin's effectiveness is excellent and serves to lift the spirits of everyone at Carville, it's one more positive thing going our way. There is a dance and theater production in Stanley's honor this evening that the entire population of Carville will attend.

***

Jenny and her special friend dance the night away, it's clear the pair are smitten with each other and I give them their privacy. It's time I turn in and make some decisions of my own.

I have a secret; I've been free from Hansen's disease for twelve months in a row. This means that I am free to leave if I so desire. I haven't told Jenny yet because I know she will want me to leave at once. But leaving her behind is something I'm not sure I can do. She's as much a part of me as my right arm now, even though she has a boyfriend and will be spending more time with him, surely she'll need me and I want to be here for her.

William is anxious to have me discharged. He wants me to live with him in New Orleans and has even asked for my hand in marriage. How ironic that I took his last name, Cooper, for my own all those years ago when I first came to Carville. I love this man with all of my heart. It's a different kind of love than what I shared with Bradley. With William things are simple, unhurried, and low key. He is my dearest friend and greatest confidant. We have nothing to hide and nothing to prove. We are just two people in love, doing our best in the eyes of God, striving to bring out the best in each other. With Bradley we had everything to lose so everything was rushed and heightened.

"Faith, Faith, are you in here?" Jenny calls out.

"In my room, dear," I answer. I dry my eyes quickly so she doesn't know I've been crying.

"Michael kissed me!" she exclaims.

"Your first kiss, how was it?" I ask. Jenny sits on my bed, cozied up next to me with her head on my shoulder.

"It was dreamy," she laughs and collapses on my bed. "What was your first kiss like?" she wants to know.

"Believe it or not, my first kiss was with William. He would come to call for me at our home and ask my parents' permission to escort me on a walk. Of course I'd gotten to know him a little at the débutante balls by this time. The balls were so grand, the gowns and the food, it was ostentatious and divine. Anyway, when he came to call, we would walk under the stars and once or twice he'd hold my hand. I remember the first time he pulled me behind a tree, away from the streetlights, and kissed me. It sent shivers up and down my spine. When he kissed me I went weak in the knees, I still do." I admit.

"What was it like with Bradley?"

"Bradley and I couldn't keep our hands off each other!" I admit, smiling at the memory.

"Do you love William?"

"I do. He's asked me to marry him, Jenny. What do you think about that?"

"I think you should do it. When you're discharged you can move in with him and then when I'm discharged I'll come live with you until I'm established as a teacher."

"What about your mother, and your boyfriend?"

"Oh," she pauses and a dreadful look crosses her face, "I didn't think about my mother, how awful of me."

"I've raised you for the last twelve years of your life, it's a natural instinct to think of me and I am flattered. I know if the tables were turned that Hope wouldn't hesitate to stay with your mother."

"Will you claim her as your own and bring her to live with you and William?"

"I would like to try, if your mother agrees. We'll see how it goes and pray she comes out of her shell," I say.

"She will."

"Jenny, I have to tell you something. I've been cleared for release."

"When?" Jenny asks, thrilled for me.

"Last week, I don't want to go without you, I can't stand the thought of you alone here."

"Oh for heaven's sake, you have to go! I have Michael and my students. I am praying for release soon anyway. You know I've been inactive for nine months now."

"I know, dear, but I just want to be here for you, if you need anything."

"I can always ring you if I need to, stop this nonsense. You would want me to go wouldn't you?"

"I suppose I would."

"I wish I could be at the wedding though."

"What a wonderful idea! You can be my maid of honor, we'll get you out on a guest pass for a few days. I know the doctors will agree!"

"It's settled then?"

"I have some packing to do, but I guess it's settled. Thank you."

I ring William in the morning and tell him I will be ready by the weekend. He wastes no time making arrangements to pick me up and promises to have everything ready at home too.

Home, what a lovely word. It's not just a place, but a feeling in my heart when I think about my steady William.

JENNY

CHAPTER 35

NUPTIALS

My Auntie Faith is getting married to William on New Years day, 1947. I am granted a leave for the occasion and am tickled to be her maid of honor. My dress is peach colored and knee length with padded shoulders and a nipped waste that hugs me in all the right places, enhancing my figure. My heels are going to be dyed to match and rhinestones will be glued on the strap. Sandy, our resident seamstress, is seeing to all of the details.

Michael has agreed to accompany me to the wedding, but he has forewarned me that it will be difficult to keep his hands to himself when I am looking so glamorous. When the big day arrives, he is looking rather dapper himself so the feeling is mutual.

The ceremony is an intimate affair that is being held right in William's back yard. He hired a crew to set up a decorative white arbor, laden with flowers, for the bride to walk through on her way to a canopy put in place to shield her from the sun during the nuptials. His rose garden has been pruned, weeded, and mulched and that's where the photos will be taken.

My entire family is in attendance. I haven't seen my siblings in nearly twelve years and I am a ball of nerves. Sally and her husband arrive first. Sally doesn't hesitate to embrace me, she apologizes profusely over and over for telling the teacher on me so long ago. To this day she blames herself for my misfortune. I assure her my containment was never her fault and that someone would have found out sooner or later, but the burden of guilt she has carried all the years shows itself in the slope of her shoulders and sad look in her eyes. She introduces me to her husband, he is an older gentleman but he appears to make her happy.

My older brother, Sam, arrives soon after Sally. He is married with two daughters under the age of six. Sam and I were never close as children because of our age gap but I am honored that he has taken time from his busy life to be here now. He is not afraid to hug me and I relish his strong embrace. His daughters, my nieces, are precious. His wife is a little standoffish, but I'll give her the benefit of the doubt. It's a strange scenario and she strikes me as cautious, not rude.

My mother and father finally arrive with the rest of the family and I am embarrassed to say but I don't even recognize Joey or Michael. They were just babies when I was sent away and now they are both fine young men. Nolan, who was seven the last time I saw him, even has a beard! He lifts me in his arms and spins me around until I am dizzy and ask to be put down. He is as feisty and devilish now as he was as a child. Memories of him chasing me around our backyard come back to me in full force now. I've missed him. I'm startled the most by Michael, he and Danny were the spitting image of one another. He has kind, blueish-gray eyes, dimples that offset his crooked smile, and a full head of blondish hair. This is what Danny would have looked like if he had survived. My heart melts and I feel guilt creep in, guilt that Michael lost his twin on my watch. Joey and Michael approach me too, they both kiss my cheeks and hug me tenderly. I know I've been missed and kept alive in their hearts all these years. I owe my mother a debt of gratitude for that.

Hope clings to my mother's skirt and hides behind her backside. I attempt to pull her out of her shell, kneeling down to her at eye level in order to say hello, but the harder I try the more visibly uncomfortable she becomes.

"She just needs time to warm up," my mother says placing a protective arm around the child.

I don't press the issue with Hope and give her the space she needs. I spend the morning making up for lost time with my family. Everyone gets along well with Michael, especially my father. The two men enjoy cigars on the carefully manicured lawn and look like they are deep in conversation.

A few of William's friends from work arrive and stand around drinking beverages and eating the finger food that was put out for their enjoyment. I believe that everyone who was invited is now here. It's time for me to check on the bride. No one from her family will be in attendance, although they were all invited.

"Faith, are you in here?" I ask peeking into the guest room upstairs.

"Come in," she says. Standing before me is one of the loveliest, most gracious women I have ever seen, made even more beautiful if it's possible. Her hair is curled in soft tendrils that frame her face. She is wearing a floor length, ivory colored, silk and lace gown that has a flattering sweetheart neckline. The sleeves are full length and come to a point just above her wrist. It's no mistake that she chose to cover the scars on her arms for this special occasion. It's her new beginning after all.

"You look stunning, Faith," I can't help but shed a few tears and worry that if I don't stop I'll ruin my makeup.

"Thank you, and you look radiant, the dress fits you perfectly. Has Michael seen it yet?" she asks.

"He has, but he's been occupied, which is a good thing. He told me it would be hard to behave himself seeing me all dolled up," I laugh.

"Is this really happening?" Faith asks me.

"It is, and I'll be by your side, as you've been by mine. It will be a memorable day, Faith, thank you for letting me be a part of it."

"I have something for you." Faith reaches into the side table drawer and pulls out a small gift box. She hands it over to me and tells me to open it.

I open the box and inside is a sterling silver infinity necklace with two tiny pearls on either side of the symbol. The pearls are representative of us, the symbol of our friendship and deep abiding love.

"You are a remarkable young woman, Jenny, and I have been so honored to have you in my life for all of these years. I don't know what brought us together, call it fate or destiny if you will, but I know in my heart you are the daughter I will never have, the sister I never had. I will love you always and forever."

My eyes flood and my makeup smears but I don't care. I am overwhelmed with feelings of love for this woman who took me under her wing.

"I know this sounds silly, but perhaps we're soul mates?" I say to Faith thinking how compatible we are even though we aren't lovers.

"It's not silly at all. I have a deep affinity and respect for you and our friendship is on an entirely different level than most, so perhaps we are," she smiles. We embrace for a moment and then retreat to the bathroom to fix our makeup and hair.

It's not long before we hear the music playing and Faith's special escort arrives to give her away. Dr. Jo, our champion physician, the man who is always in our corner whispering words of encouragement, has come here for the blessed event. He looks striking in his suit and tie and it's nice to see him in something other than his white doctor's coat. His wife is in attendance also as an honored guest. Without her support Dr. Jo would never have been able to be so devoted to his cause.

He takes Faith's elbow in his hands and leads her down the stairway, through the family room, out the back door. Her groom is standing and waiting rather impatiently under the canopy. I walk before Faith carrying a simple bouquet made of baby's breath and soft peach colored roses. I spread her train when she is in position beside William and take her bouquet and mesh it with my own.

The ceremony is over in ten minutes; there is not a dry eye among us, even my father uses his hanky to wipe his eyes and nose. We are observing a special union, it's true, but we're also celebrating Faith's plight and now her freedom.

Faith won't be going back to Carville with me. She has been fully discharged and finally has the chance to live the life she always dreamed with her first love.

I keep my eyes on Hope during the afternoon and pray she warms up, but it is apparent to everyone that she is only truly comfortable with the woman who raised her. My heart breaks for Faith; I remember when she turned to me after she named her baby, Hope, and said, "all we need now is love."

I feel doubly blessed to have two incredible women in my life and not a day passes that I don't thank God for the blessing. I pray Hope comes around and feels this way some day too.

CHAPTER 36

TORN

The Public Health Service removed Hansen's disease from the list of quarantinable diseases this year. This means anyone that is granted a short leave from Carville no longer requires a travel permit or permission from each township they enter.

I was granted a pass for Faith's wedding three months ago and today I received the excellent, heartening news I've been praying for. I have been discharged altogether. My blood smears have been free from any Hansen's bacteria for twelve solid months in a row. If there is such a thing as survivor's guilt, then I surely have it. Why do I get to leave when so many others don't?

The only thorn in my side is that I will have to take Dapsone pills for the rest of my life. They are supposed to keep the disease at bay so that I can live normally. I am certain, however, they have a host of side effects like all the other medications I've been on over the years. These side effects are more diverse and can range from vertigo, tinnitus, dizziness, ringing in the ears, and heart palpitations, to serious problems with blood and liver that can be fatal.

Guilt overwhelms me when I think of people like Dorothy who don't stand a chance. If she were ever discharged what on earth would she do? Who would take care of her outside of the fence? She is so disfigured that she would be ridiculed and stared at. For people like her, Carville is a place of refuge, not reproach. It's a safe haven away from a cruel society.

I ring Faith and share my good news. She is beside herself that I get to 'come home' now.

"You never gave up hope, Jenny. Not once did you complain this whole time, not once. I am so proud of you. Have you told

Michael yet?"

"Not yet, you were my first call. I have to call Jane now and then I will deliver the news in person to Michael."

"Good luck. I love you," she says before hanging up.

When I call my mother a child answers the phone, "Hope, is that you?"

"This is Hope, who's calling please?" she asks.

"This is Jenny, how are you, darling?"

"Fine, thank you," she says and then hands the phone over. She is cordial, but not personable.

"Jenny? Is everything okay?" my mother asks.

"I have good news, I have been discharged! I am free of the disease, Mother, can you believe it?"

"Congratulations. You have been so patient, what will you do now, where will you go?" she wants to know.

"I am not sure, I only just found out. I need to give it some thought. Michael's job is here, but golly, I want to get out and see the world," I admit.

"Well, you know that you are always welcome here, we would love to have you. I understand, though, if you want to live somewhere more cosmopolitan like New Orleans. That would delight Faith."

"I know it would, it's all happening so fast. Give my love to everyone and I'll be in touch." We chat for a few minutes about my dad and brothers and when I hang up the phone my heart feels pulled in two different directions. I am torn.

Michael and I meet up for our daily afternoon walk. His work day ends at four p.m. and mine ends at three, so we usually spend the afternoons together and then part before supper.

"Hello, beautiful," Michael says to me as he approaches.

"Hi. I have some news."

"Well, go on then, spill it," he encourages, patience is not one of his strong suits.

"I have been given my discharge papers!"

Michael doesn't hesitate for one second before dropping down on one knee and proposing! It's so unexpected that I'm not sure what's happening.

"I spoke with your father at Faith's wedding. He has given me his blessing and permission to ask for your hand. Jenny, I adore you, I admire you, and I love you. Will you make me the happiest man in the world and marry me?"

"Yes!" I shout for everyone to hear. We kiss and hug and behave like children we are so excited.

"You have spent twelve years here, I'm sure you'll want to get out of this place and live somewhere new, am I right?"

"Well, I've grown attached to my students, and I know you like your job, so that's a consideration. However, if I'm being honest I'd like to get as far away from this place as we can. I have so much to see and do and now that I'm free I want to experience it all."

"I want to experience it with you. I will put in my two-week notice tomorrow. Now that you're discharged I'd like you to meet my family."

"Do they know about me? I mean that I had leprosy?"

"My parents do, but my siblings don't. Since you're healthy it doesn't matter either way."

"That's true, I just worry they won't want to be around me. They might be afraid of me."

"Not my folks, they aren't like that. Are you free for supper with them tomorrow night?"

"Let me check my schedule," I tease. "Why of course I'm free, silly."

We hold hands for a nice long walk and when we return I immediately call Faith to share the news.

"He proposed," I shout into the phone before she even has time to say hello.

"Congratulations, how exciting. I am sure he'll make you very happy."

"Thank you. I know he will. He's charming and handsome, but more importantly he works hard and will be a good provider for my family. My gosh, this means I could actually have a family of my own now."

"Yes you can! May I ask you something?"

"Always."

"You can say no, but I wonder if you'd like to wear my wedding gown?"

"Oh my goodness, yes, yes I would!" I am beyond excited because Faith's gown is stunning.

"You can alter it anyway you want, it's my gift to you."

"Thank you. Faith, for everything."

Part of me wants to have a small ceremony right here at Carville so Dorothy can be a bridesmaid, but I know people from the outside might be uncomfortable coming here. Michael and I discuss it and decide we'll have two ceremonies, one here and one in New Orleans.

Stanley Stein is anxious to post my news in his paper and as a result the article he writes many folks volunteer to help. The gardening club offers to make my bouquet and all the arrangements for my tables. The kitchen staff is happy to prepare my favorite meal, chicken fricassee, for everyone in attendance. A few younger ladies work at the salon and they are already clipping photos of up-do's that might be nice for my day. The bakery shop on campus is going to make my cake, the choir is going to sing, the band is going to be the entertainment and several other folks have offered to help with the set up and take down of all the tables and chairs we'll need.

Everyone is excited, except for Dorothy. Dorothy is morose and I empathize with her. I ask her to be a bridesmaid and that makes her a little more jovial, but her depression has more to do with the fact that she doesn't think she'll have a chance at love because of the way she looks. She is in rehabilitation for her legs, is blind, and now she has painful ulcers that have spread across her face. It's painful to watch and a feeling of deep regret regarding her situation overwhelms me.

CHAPTER 37

WOMANHOOD

I am a married woman, emphasis on 'woman' as a result of my glorious wedding night. I had no idea that such pleasure could exist between a man and woman. I had heard people talk about sex as if it were an obligation and unwelcome duty, for me it's completely the opposite. I find it rather enjoyable and I am an active participant.

When Michael undresses me at night I relish his warm, soft touch. He covers me with kisses and caresses my body until I can no longer stand it and willingly open my legs for him. We fit together perfectly, like a jigsaw puzzle, and although our lovemaking is different every time it's always satisfying for both of us.

Michael has revealed himself to be a regular Casanova! He brings me flowers and candy, plies me with wine and spirits for no other reason than he loves me and feels I deserve to be pampered.

After much deliberation we decide to make New Orleans our home. We rent a small apartment that's only seven miles away from Faith and William's home. We have a standing dinner date with them every Sunday afternoon and speak by phone at least three times a week. William's law practice is booming now and Faith helps him in the office from nine a.m. to three in the afternoon Monday through Thursday. She's busy living life to the fullest, which gives me great hope and pleasure.

They are trying for a baby, but so far they have not had any luck. I on the other hand, am sure I'm with child. My nipples are sore when they rub against my brassiere and I've been nauseous in the mornings. I haven't told Faith because I worry it will make her feel sad.

Michael is working as a clerk at a drugstore for the time being and I am tutoring children who need extra help after school. Life is grand. I have everything I've ever dreamed and more. I am not spiteful as a result of all the time I missed in the outside world, instead I choose to believe God put me in Carville for several reasons, one was to meet Faith, my forever friend, and another, to meet Michael, my lover.

CHAPTER 38

DOROTHY

It's already 1950, time has flown by. Over the past three years I have done my best to visit Dorothy whenever I am able. But, I admit that this time I am a tad overdue. Life has gotten in the way and I have my son to think of now. Charlie is the light of my life, but he is a precocious little devil that I can't take my eyes off of for a second. Michael encourages his naughty behavior and tells me to lighten up, but I can't have a child run the household for heaven's sake!

We'd like to have more children if we are able, but Charlie was a difficult pregnancy. I developed very high blood pressure and was put on bed rest for the entire last trimester. Faith was a Godsend during that time and I hope to repay the favor in kind because she is now pregnant with twins. So far she is healthy and the pregnancy is going well, but I know she'll need my help when the little ones are born.

For my trip to Carville I have packed all kinds of specialty items for Dorothy and my teacher friends, and even have a few dozen books to donate to the library.

It's been sometime since I've been back here on the expansive grounds and the first thing I notice upon my arrival is that the twelve foot barbed wire fence that surrounded the property has been taken down at long last. Carville is no longer a prison that keeps people locked inside, but a community in and of itself. That gigantic, looming eyesore is finally in a dump where it belongs.

Nowadays things have really changed at Carville. Twenty new patients arrived from the Virgin Islands recently, adding to the cultural diversity and overall environment for the patients. I've been told that a dozen or more patients are working on obtaining bachelor's degrees in a variety of fields, proving they feel hopeful even in the face of adversity. There is talk that marriage will be sanctioned soon and couples will be permitted to live together in the small homes on Cottage Row on Main Street. More important is the fact that twelve months of negative labs are no longer necessary for discharge. The ethics committee established an entirely new set of rules; first and foremost before any patient is discharged, their ability to support themselves in the real world must be established. There must not be any children in residence where they are going, and they must agree to take their Dapsone pills regularly for the rest of their lives.

Even though Carville has made numerous strides, many patients still suffer under the weight of Hansen's. It can take an emotional toll as well as a physical toll and with every sunrise the folks have to muster the energy to face a new day.

Dorothy is frail and sickly when I enter her room in the house that's been established for the blind. She is accustomed to living without eye sight, but is still adjusting to the fact her legs have been amputated. Her empty pant legs cover her stumps and flap against each other making a whooshing sound as she turns towards the sound of her door opening. The doctor says she is healing well, but her spirits are down. I've brought a small radio as a gift and turn it on, normally she would tap her feet in time with the tune, but today she just sits in her wheelchair and cocks her ear towards the speaker and listens. It's the small pleasures and gifts that mean the most to her now.

"Hello my friend, it's me, Jenny," I say while tucking her pants under so they are more comfortable.

She reaches her hands out in front of her and I grab them to mine, her claw-like fingers are cold and bony. I embrace her tightly and shower her with love.

"How are you?" I ask.

"Tired."

"Dorothy, I've discussed it with Michael and we'd like you to consider living with us."

"That's very generous, Jenny. I would surely like to meet your little fella, but this is my home. I'll never leave."

"You just don't seem happy and I want to help."

"Oh, I'm fine and dandy. I'm just aging faster than most, but if I'm honest I like it here, I feel safe. I have friends and people to do things with. We play Bingo every Wednesday and someone always wheels me to the baseball games and movies. Some of the girls take turns reading to me now, it's delightful to hear their sweet voices. I'm fine, really and truly. You caught me having an off moment that's all."

"Well, you're certainly entitled to those. Let's go for a walk," I suggest.

I put a shawl across my oldest and dearest friend's shoulders and wheel her outside. It's quieter here than it used to be, but I think it's because people aren't spending their time milling around. Now it seems everyone has a job or an activity they are heavily immersed in.

"It's strange to be back, I grew up here. So few will ever understand what that was like. People can be so cruel, but never once was anyone mean or rude to me when I lived here. There are actually things about it that I miss."

"Like what?"

"Like the Carville cheese, it's superior to anything else I've ever tasted."

"The ice cream too, and the fricassee," she reminds me.

"Yes! Do they still make that every other Tuesday?"

"They do."

We chatter on like a couple of old hens all afternoon long. When Dorothy is tuckered out I take her back to her accommodations and hug her goodbye.

There is something I need to do that can't wait any longer. I borrow a pair of sheers from the kitchen and walk towards the fragrant, blooming gardens. The Coca Cola bottles outlining the flowers reflect and dance in the sun's rays. I cut a few snips of roses, daisies, and black-eyed Susans and walk across the campus to the cemetery. I'm lost in thought remembering my little brother.

My baby brother's grave was never properly marked and that's one thing I'd like to rectify. The stigma and fear people had was so great that a small child's grave had to go unmarked, his life unrecognized. I can't help but feel there's an injustice in that. I know how to find him though, he's the third stone in the third row closest to the lake. This helped me when I was little because it was easy to remember. My family has never come to pay their respects, they do that their own way I suppose.

I lay the flowers on the stone and pull the weeds that have grown up along side it.

"Hello, Danny boy. I miss you."

I sit and reflect on my time here, wondering how Danny's life would have turned out if he had survived the disease. If he were born later when Promin was available he would have had a chance for survival. I can't take the past back, but I can do something about the future.

I walk to the farm and inquire with the fellows if anyone knows a mason that can make me a proper memorial. I want a stone carver with an artistic eye. I am given contact information for a fellow that lives outside of town. I give him a ring and discuss what I'd like for my brother's grave. I want his name in bold letters so everyone knows who he was, I want the date he lived and the date he died, I also want a quote. I am choosing between several bible versus; Psalm 9:9, The LORD is a refuge for the oppressed, a stronghold in times of trouble. Or Psalm 22:24, For he has not despised or disdained the suffering of the afflicted one; he has not hidden his face from him but has listened to his cry for help.

This is my gift to Danny, it's small and only a few people will ever see it, but I will know his headstone will be marked. Now everyone will be able to see there once lived a lovable little boy named Danny who died from leprosy.

FAITH

CHAPTER 39

FAITH 1952

My sister, Emily, died. She was only thirty-three when it happened, but I'm told it was from natural causes. I've not been in touch with my biological family at all since my discharge, choosing to live among those who love and support me versus those who shun me.

"I'm struggling, William, do I attend the funeral or not?"

"That's entirely up to you, you know I will support whatever you decide."

That's my husband, supportive and caring, but never one to make decisions, he leaves those to me.

"Well then, I think I should go. I'll stand in the back and pay my respects quietly."

"You're not going alone, the boys and I will come too."

"I'm not sure I want the boys to come. They are probably too young. My parents wouldn't recognize them if they fell over them on the street. It's selfish but I almost don't want them to see the boys and I certainly don't want them to introduce themselves as the boys' grandparents. That would be too confusing."

"That's not like you, Faith, darling."

"Ugh, and that's another thing, they'll call me Frances and that's such an uptight name, maybe I should stay home after all."

"Look, we'll ask Jenny if she can watch the boys, Charlie will look forward to having some playmates, and we'll be back in a couple of days."

"Okay, I'll start packing."

***

My mother is hardly recognizable, it's been over fifteen years since I've laid eyes on her and time has not been her friend. She is obese now and harsh looking. Her make up is fiercely applied and she wears a scowl across her face that scares the daylights out of me.

My father is next to a younger, fashionable, woman and I realize they're holding hands. Is it the secretary? I wonder, remembering the affair from so long ago.

I am reluctant to be seen, so William and I sneak into a pew in the back of the church. We have been given a program and inside it there is a notification that donations can be made to the American Cancer Society. I would assume, then, that my sister died from a form of cancer. I pray she didn't suffer.

When the service is over and the family members leave the church everyone mingles in the lobby making it difficult to sneak out unnoticed. My mother spots me first. Her chubby hand goes to her mouth and her instincts force her take a step backwards.

Nothing has changed in all of these years. It doesn't matter that the disease is no longer quarantinable or contagious, to my mother I will always be a dirty leper. For heaven's sake it's common knowledge now that leprosy is derived from armadillos, of all things.

William witnesses the charade and places his arm across my shoulders, guiding me outdoors and into our car. In that moment I realize that my family is not from blood. My family is from shared experiences, mutual respect, love and understanding.

I refuse to shed even a single tear today, and instead we enjoy a quiet supper at a local restaurant and stay in a warm and cozy hotel room for the night. We'll make the night about us; and our ability to overcome obstacles. He holds a glass of champagne to mine and we toast to one another, and to our true family.

DOROTHY

CHAPTER 40

DOROTHY 1996

I am one of the last lepers residing at the place that was formerly known as Carville. I came here in 1930 when I was only six years old. I was dropped at the front gate like so many before and after me. I am not sure if Dorothy is the name I was given at birth, or if it was picked out for me the second I became a patient at the Leper Home.

I remember that my ears were scabby and sometimes they itched. My mother would slap my hands and tell me to stop itching. She would even cover my hands in socks so I didn't break the skin. She mistook my lesions for poor hygiene and scrubbed my ears, neck, and scalp with Brillo. When that did little to remedy my patches, she treated me for lice. She frantically washed all our sheets and pillowcases in scalding water, but I still itched. The scabs fell off over time, but then small pustules formed where they had been.

I can't recall going to the doctor, but I must have and I'm sure it cost my mother a pretty penny that she didn't have to spare.

I don't remember a lot about the woman who gave birth to me, there is a shadow where her face should be. I have glimpses of what I think might be memories spent with her, but I'll never know for sure. I know she was only sixteen years old when she had me. I don't remember a daddy, that doesn't mean I didn't have one, but my mind draws a blank wherever he is concerned.

I didn't have much with me when I arrived, so the kindly nuns took me under their wings as a charity case. They made sure I had clothing and toilette articles. I was put in a dormitory specially designed for the children here. Boys were in one hall and girls were in the other. I had a roommate named Marilyn, she was an older girl and I followed her everywhere. She had the patience of a saint and was always kind towards me up until the day she died. I was ten and it was my first real experience with death.

Shortly after her passing, a new girl close to my age arrived. Her birth name was Jenny, but her Carville name was Diane. She let me call her Jenny though because she thought Diane was too dowdy. We became fast friends and soon everyone referred to us as "the girls". "Are the girls at lunch?" or, "Are the girls interested in going to the movies tonight, they are playing the Wizard of Oz."

Jenny had a mother who came to visit as often as she could. Sometimes I would go with her to the fence and say hello. Over the years, Jenny's mother started packing small gifts for me, just little things like socks and underwear, a new toothbrush, hair clips, and hair ribbons. It was more than I received elsewhere so I was always grateful. I wrote thank you letters to Jane, that's her name, and eventually she and I became pen pals. It was incredible to be in touch with someone from the outside world.

Jenny met a special friend named Faith, I know that's her Carville name, and she also took me under her wing. I had so many people taking care of me when I was little that eventually I forgot to miss my mother. Carville became my home and I have lived here for sixty-six years!

In all this time, one of my favorite memories was in 1950 when everyone gathered to watch a submarine pass through the river. Nearly everyone from Carville, staff and patients alike, were present for the event. We made it into a grand party that lasted long into the night.

The facility came under scrutiny a few years back when certain folks in government wanted it shut down. They felt the hospital was no longer useful as a result of experimentation and trials as well as the introduction of the sulfone drug, Promin, that slowly reversed symptoms. Medical advances like this were a beacon of hope for the younger patients and those with fewer outward symptoms. But for someone like me with an aggressive form of the disease, I cringed at the thought of the facility closing.

Luckily for those of us with rotting limbs, ulcers, facial deformities, and blindness, Gillis W. Long lobbied on our behalf and was able to pass a bill through Congress that entitled us to live out our lives here, in the comfort of our home. We were given a choice between a long term nursing care facility in Baton Rouge, or a thirty-three dollar annual stipend to help us live out our days comfortably on campus.

The facility was even renamed the, Gillis W. Long Hansen's Disease (Leprosy) Center in 1986 in honor of the man who fought for us.

I don't feel like a leper here, here I am just plain old Dorothy. In the 80s there were still four hundred staff members and just as many patients receiving treatment on campus. I am not an outcast whatsoever. No one sizes me up or asks questions about my legs, people don't treat me differently or make me feel ugly. I couldn't survive anywhere else. When Jenny invited me to live with her I was touched, but declined. I would never burden her with all of my needs. I require more care than most, but the Sisters have been more than gracious to me over the years tirelessly addressing my bandages and feeding me. I was moved into the blind house years ago and look forward to the sounds of the squeaky food carts bringing us our dinner.

When the facility became a federal prison in 1990, it made me uncomfortable to feel prying eyes graze my mangled form and cringe. Eventually the felons got to know us and some of us even became friends if you can believe it. I can't think of a harsher punishment for a criminal than being placed in a facility with a bunch of lepers! The prison was in operation for three years and then closed down, I don't know why although I suspect it had to do with funding, but it was abrupt.

I spend my days working at the museum now. It was founded earlier this year, 1996. The Gillis W. Long Hansen's Disease (Leprosy) Center was moved to Baton Rouge where they will continue to research the disease and provide clinical care for anyone who needs it. The long term goal is to eradicate Hansen's Disease all together by the year 2000. If I have played some small part in that goal then I have served my time well and done my duty as a Christian. I understand there are still people who carry the disease, but providing they take their medication and receive follow up treatment, they will be in remission and not contagious to anyone.

People travel from far and wide to come to the museum. Some had family members that stayed here for a stint and are interested in understanding their lives, others are students from universities studying social structures. Still others are interested in richly detailed medical histories and patients' rights. We do our best to provide as much detailed information as we can about the changes that took place here, using exhibits. For instance, there is an exhibit of the "Carville sandal", the shoe that was designed specifically to help patients with deformed feet walk more comfortably. We recreated patient dormitories and bedrooms complete with hanging artwork, photos, games like Dominoes that were often played, and original furnishings. We have lots of memorabilia in the way of photographs and newspaper articles for people to read and learn from too. We even have a few Mardi Gras floats and artifacts from the parades, this usually surprises tourists the most. We adhere to strict guidelines about patient privacy, using nicknames whenever discussing a specific case.

Unfortunately, the original antebellum mansion is not tourable. It's still in use, but houses federal offices now rather than the administration offices it used to. Our main goal in establishing the museum was to show this incredible self-sustaining property and its fascinating time line, but especially to showcase the strides taken here to obliterate leprosy. Leprosy was the first bacterial disease ever to be discovered and that's quite an accomplishment.

The word on the street is that the control of the site will be transferred from the United States Public Health Service to the State of Louisiana. The state has high hopes they will be able use the grounds and facilities to mentor troubled youth and teach them job skills. I could tell them a thing or two about not wasting your life!

The most astounding thing that has happened in all of my years occurred at the church. On several occasions I have entered and heard the voices of the Sisters' choir singing. I don't have eyesight and rely heavily on my other senses. I have been told that every time I thought I heard the lovely music, no one was actually singing. Later, I found out I wasn't alone in hearing the voices. Those of us here believe that what we hear are angels singing. The chapel has been sanctified by the struggles of hundreds of hearts that poured out daily before God. To this day people say they hear the music and I can think of no more deserving souls, than those at Carville.